"I'm going to kiss you."

"Shane, I don't think—"

"Shhh."

"But—"

"You think too much."

Damn it. Why did he have to be Shane Gillian, a famous bull rider with a career as demanding as hers? And why did she have to be Kaitlin Cooper, born with racing in her blood? And then she admitted he was right. She thought too much.

"Let's go home."

But it wasn't her home. It would never be her home. And he wasn't her husband. Well, not really. In name only.

"I can't. Please don't kiss me again. Not until we have this all figured out. We're only making things more difficult."

"Kait—"

"No. We can talk in the morning."

"Why not now?"

Because she was too conflicted. Because when he touched her she didn't know which way was up. Because for the first time in her life she felt herself falling for someone.

And it scared her to death.

Dear Reader,

Years ago I wrote a series of romance novels centered on stock car racing. I've always loved those books, but it wasn't until a friend of mine said, "Hey. You ought to write a book about a female race-car driver who falls in love with a cowboy," that I thought, "Eureka!"

And so you might recognize my heroine, Kaitlin Cooper. She's the daughter of Lance and Sarah Cooper, my first stock-car-racing couple. It's pretty crazy how certain characters are like family, so when Kaitlin ends up pregnant, well, I knew fireworks would fly with her mom and dad. Throw in a cowboy son-in-law and, well...NASCAR royalty is in for a rocky ride.

And poor Shane Gillian. One spectacular night changes his life forever. He can't decide if that's a good thing or bad. All he knows is fate has given him the chance to woo the woman of his dreams...and he only hopes he's up to the task.

As always, I hope you enjoy the tale. I hope those of you who have followed me since my stock-car-racing days are pleased. It was a joy to revisit some of my favorite characters from the racing world. Thank you for your patience.

By the way, that friend of mine? She really *is* a female race-car driver and she really *did* fall in love with a professional cowboy. Sometimes truth is stranger than fiction.

All my best,

Pamela

RODEO LEGENDS: SHANE

PAMELA BRITTON

HARLEQUIN® WESTERN ROMANCE

Recycling programs
for this product may
not exist in your area.

ISBN-13: 978-1-335-69960-2

Rodeo Legends: Shane

Copyright © 2018 by Pamela Britton

Printed in U.S.A.

With more than a million books in print, **Pamela Britton** likes to call herself the best-known author nobody's ever heard of. Of course, that changed thanks to a certain licensing agreement with that little racing organization known as NASCAR.

But before the glitz and glamour of NASCAR, Pamela wrote books that were frequently voted the best of the best by the *Detroit Free Press*, Barnes & Noble (two years in a row) and *RT Book Reviews*. She's won numerous awards, including a National Readers' Choice Award and a nomination for the Romance Writers of America Golden Heart® Award.

When not writing books, Pamela is a reporter for a local newspaper. She's also a columnist for the *American Quarter Horse Journal*.

Books by Pamela Britton

Harlequin Western Romance

Cowboys in Uniform

Her Rodeo Hero
His Rodeo Sweetheart
The Ranger's Rodeo Rebel
Her Cowboy Lawman
Winning the Rancher's Heart

Visit the Author Profile page
at Harlequin.com for more titles.

For Evelynn Brooks,
the inspiration for this story.
No, I didn't make my heroine tall, dark and
gorgeous. But I did make her kindhearted,
talented and funny...just like you.
Wishing you years of joy and happiness
with your own handsome cowboy.

Chapter One

Kaitlin Cooper stared down at the plastic tube sitting on the counter of her bathroom, the twin lines of pink an evil eye that seemed to glare up at her.

"No," she murmured, clutching the counter for support. But the two lines were unmistakable. Still, she picked the tube up, turning it this way and that, hoping against hope the pink lines were a trick of the light. They weren't.

Pregnant. That was what the little diagram for dummies told her.

How did this happen?

She straightened, tipped her head back. Well, she knew *how*. But she took precautions. She *had* to take precautions. Stock-car racing was a male-dominated sport. All she needed were rumors of a pregnancy to unravel all the hard work she'd put into her career.

Pregnant.

Her fingernails started to ache. Only then did she take a deep breath, straighten up and firmly look herself in the eye. Her pupils were like tiny dots in blots of blue paint. Her blond hair, usually pulled back in a ponytail, hung loose around her shoulders slightly mussed, not surprising since she'd run her fingers through the long strands at least a half a dozen times while waiting for the pregnancy test to reveal its grim news.

Okay. So. She was pregnant. She'd figure out the pros and cons.

Pros: she now had an explanation for the sudden bouts of dizziness and the persistent stomach flu that had refused to go away. She wasn't suffering the lingering effects of concussion. She wasn't terminally ill. She was going to have a baby.

Con: *she was going to have a baby.*

Her sponsor would freak. She couldn't race while pregnant, which meant she'd have to break the news to the team owner, who just so happened to be her dad, and she didn't even want to *think* about how that little conversation would go. Plus she had a race in two weeks, the first race of the season. How would they find a replacement driver in time?

She leaned over the sink because she truly felt she might vomit.

How did it happen?

Duh. She'd had a quick fling with Shane Gillian, professional rodeo rider, a man she'd met in Las Vegas. He'd been there for the National Finals Rodeo. She'd been there to test her new car. They'd both been invited to the same party. They'd hit it off comparing notes about life on the road and the pitfalls of fame. Heck, they both had famous fathers, too, and, well, one thing had led to another, and she couldn't even blame it on stupidity brought on by an overindulgence of alcohol. It had just…happened.

Dumb, dumb, dumb.

She padded back to her bedroom. Her eyes caught on the massive bed in the center of the room. Her own little slice of heaven with its off-white bedspread and fluffy pillows. All she wanted to do was climb beneath the covers and pull them over her head. Her fingers shook as she automatically reached for the cell phone sitting on her nightstand. Still, she hesitated. She could always just deal with this on her own. Shane Gillian didn't need to know. She could make an announcement detailing her need to take a break from racing...

She *couldn't* take a break. People just didn't quit for a year. What would her fans say? Scratch that. What would her *mother* say?

Her eyes began to burn, but she refused to cry. She hated crybabies. Race-car drivers were made of sterner stuff. She just needed to figure something out.

Her fingers scanned the contact list in her phone without her even thinking about it, and the name Shane Gillian appeared right there in black and white. She hadn't called him...afterward. She'd assumed he, like her, had a busy life. He hadn't called her, either. It'd been a fling. They'd both known that. Never mind the connection they'd had. Things might have turned out differently if they were different people with different careers and different lives. But they'd both known what would happen the next morning. No hard feelings.

She pressed the call button. It rang once before she hung up. This kind of news should be delivered in person. *Maybe a video chat?* she thought as she plopped down on the bed. Would that work? *Beep. Beep. Guess what? We're pregnant.*

Her phone rang.

She about jumped out of her skin. A name flashed on the screen. He'd called her back.

Ignore him.

But she couldn't. If she planned to meet with him, she would need to contact him sooner or later. So she took a deep breath, told herself to calm down, closed her eyes and said, "Hey."

A deep baritone, the same one that'd sent chills up her spine the day they'd met, said, "It *is* you, isn't it? I thought it might be. Recognized the area code."

She gulped. What to say?

She opened her eyes. Stared out at the water beyond her single-story home on the shores of Lake Norman. A home she was proud of. A home she'd purchased on her own with the purse money from her first big win. It was beautiful outside. She could smell the blooms of the cherry tree from where she sat, although how the sun could still be shining when her whole world had just been turned end over end, she had no idea.

"Hello?"

"Oh, um, sorry. I didn't mean to call. I mean, I did, I just decided I'd call you later instead."

"Is this a bad time?"

She almost laughed. Hysterical laughter. Instead she said, "No, no. I can talk."

Pregnant.

Silence again. She took the plunge. "I've, ah, been thinking about you. And, um, I have some free time this weekend. I was wondering if maybe you and I could get together?"

She could perfectly picture his blue eyes. The dark hair. The sideburns. Heck, even his smile. He had the sweetest smile. It emphasized the cleft in his chin, which always seemed to be covered by the faintest hint of a beard in the pictures she'd seen of him online.

"What did you have in mind?"

Surely he could hear the panic in her voice? Or her harsh breaths? She felt on the verge of an anxiety attack. This wasn't just a mistake. This was a disaster. Potentially a career-ending disaster. She needed him to know. Needed his help.

"I could fly out to California…"

She left the rest of her words unspoken. She knew what he would think. That she wanted to see him again for another wild night of debauchery. What he couldn't know was that their night together had been a complete aberration. She didn't just fall into bed with complete strangers. She couldn't afford to do that.

"That sounds great." She could hear the smile in his voice. "I can show you my hometown."

He was the son of a famous team roper. That much she knew. Some kind of multiple world champion. She'd done a little bit of Googling after their night together. She also knew he was a bull rider. And that he was good. As good as she was at driving a race car.

No driving anymore.

Despite her best efforts, she felt a knot build in her throat. It made it hard to say, "It won't be an imposition?"

"Not at all."

She found a pen and paper, scribbled down the details, her hands shaking so badly she doubted she'd be able to read it later.

My mother is going to kill me.

She would deal with that later. Right after she talked to Shane.

Shane.

The drop-dead-gorgeous cowboy who had rocked her world.

And gotten her pregnant.

"You sure you don't want to head out to the Silver Spur later on?"

Shane glanced at his brother Carson and shook his head. Hotrod, the horse he'd been riding, liked to bloat his gut whenever he cinched him up, and Shane could see the damn leather strap was hanging like an empty noose beneath the horse's belly. *Son of a—* Good thing he hadn't fallen while they were out checking the new calves. Too damn distracted thinking about *her*.

"I hear Amber's going to be there," Carson teased.

Amber Jamison was a woman who wasn't exactly well-known for her upstanding moral conduct and who'd been chasing after Shane for as long as he could remember.

"Got plans," he told his brother, glancing at the dark-haired mirror image of their father. "Friend coming from out of town."

"Friend?"

Carson was grinning at him with a suggestive look in his eyes. His dad, Reese, had sired five Gillian kids. He came from a large family, even though his mom had died seven years ago. He had four cousins, too, not to mention assorted step-cousins thanks to his uncle's first, failed marriage to a woman with kids of her own. All of them, even the ones not related to him by blood, seemed determined to see him settle down. Little did they know. The one woman in the world who'd ever piqued his interest, someone he'd never thought he'd see again, would meet him at her hotel in less than an hour. God forbid she come here. All three of his brothers and two of his cousins shared the ranch-hand quarters, and he didn't need them to catch wind of his fling with Kaitlin Cooper.

"What's her name?" Carson asked, one of his thick

brows lifting in a teasing way. Shane slipped the bridle off his sorrel's head. The horse tried to soothe an itch on Carson's arm.

They stood out in front of a single-story twenty-four-horse barn made to match the ranch house a quarter mile down the road. They raised cutting horses and every one of the horses lived like a king in a Spanish-style barn with a terra-cotta-tile roof and a stucco exterior that reflected the sun's rays, making Shane squint beneath his cowboy hat.

"None of your business."

"None-of-Your-Business?" His brother hooked the bridle on the horn of the saddle. "I've met her before. Has a brother named Stay-Out-of-My-Business."

"That's the one."

The Gillian families shared a large area of acreage, which meant keeping a secret would be next to impossible. Everyone knew everyone's secrets when you were constantly under each other's feet. His uncle and his cousins lived off to the north, but they shared in the duties of caring for five hundred head. The land had been bought with money won at numerous rodeos, including the National Finals. His dad and his uncle had been famous team ropers. Hell, they were still famous, and they'd been smart enough to invest in land and cattle back when it'd been cheap in Via Del Caballo. He planned to settle down on a portion of it, but his dad didn't believe in simply handing things to his kids, so he was doing his best to make his own way.

You need to earn it, boy-ah.

He could perfectly hear his dad's blustery voice. So he had to win a national championship first. And pay his dad for the land. He was almost there, too, but he'd

drawn a dink in the last round of the finals last year
and lost the average by a hair. He'd still won a bag of
money, but not enough to pay his dad for the land and to
build his dream home out in the south forty. It'd about
killed him, too. He'd been drowning his sorrows when
he'd met Kaitlin in December. She'd walked into the
NFR after-party, and he'd been blown away because, of
course, he had recognized her. He'd been a fan of stock-
car racing ever since he was old enough to watch TV.

"Heellooo."

A hand blocked his view. He realized he'd paused
with his hands on the saddle, one on the cantle, the other
on the pommel, and with what was no doubt a bemused
smile on his face.

"Okay, spill." Carson slipped between him and his
horse. "Who is she and where'd you meet her?"

Shane sidestepped him, moving to the other side to
take off his saddle. The smell of the animal's wet coat
filled the air.

"Can you leave me alone?" He hid his eyes beneath
the brim of his black cowboy hat. "I'm in a hurry here."

"Come on, man." Carson followed him for a step or
two. "I'm dying to know."

He wouldn't tell him. Carson would tell his dad,
which would result in a lecture from dear old Dad on
the importance of keeping your eye on the goal.

Carson followed him into the barn and to the tack
room to the right.

"For the love of—" Shane set the saddle down on
one of the saddle racks. The room held dozens of them.
Championship saddles, all of them. The Dynamic Duo
had been his dad and uncle's team nickname. Rodeo
legends, the both of them.

"You don't need to know who it is. Besides, she'll be leaving almost as soon as she arrives, and I doubt I'll hear from her afterward. Not for a while, at least."

But if anything, the words made his brother seem even more curious. Shane refused to talk about Kaitlin, though. Just as he hadn't told Carson about the night he'd met her. They'd both done a good job keeping their one-night romance out of the limelight. He planned to keep it that way.

Still, he kept a watchful eye in his truck's rearview mirror as he drove away from the ranch a half hour later. He wouldn't put it past his brother to follow him. Carson was that way. Not a serious bone in his body. The thing was, and it irked the hell out of Shane, life just seemed to fall into place for Carson. He was a team roper like Daddy and Uncle Bob, but had he set a goal to try to make it to the NFR? Hell no. And then when he'd gotten there through blind luck, he'd just lackadaisically roped his way through each round, coming within a hairbreadth of winning the whole shebang. Meanwhile, Shane had twisted himself into knots until that final round in his event. Then he'd had the rotten luck to draw Dingo. Some things just weren't fair.

He'd traveled halfway to town before he realized the motel was only a few miles away. He'd purposely given her the name of a place on the outskirts of Via Del Caballo. The fewer prying eyes that spotted the two of them together, the better. He loved his hometown with its rolling hills—they were green this time of year—and picturesque downtown, but the thing about Via Del Caballo was that everyone knew who everyone was. Still, he felt a little guilty as he pulled into the single-story Spanish-style motel with a wooden railing and doors that opened to the parking lot. He felt about sixteen again, like a kid sneaking out to a party.

Nervous.

He had to wipe his hands on his truck's steering wheel. Crazy how many emotions were coursing through him. Excitement. Curiosity. Anticipation.

He would bet it was her rental car he'd parked next to. Sure enough, as he walked by he could see the rent-a-car sticker in the front windshield. He didn't even need to knock, either, because her motel door opened and there she was, his all-American girl with her blond hair and blue, blue eyes.

"Hey there," he said.

She smiled, but it was a forced grin, and that was his first clue that something wasn't quite right. He'd expected a sultry grin, maybe even a flirtatious comment, but instead she stepped aside, allowing him access to her room without so much as shaking his hand.

"Sit down."

His heart pumped double-time then, but not for the reason it'd been pounding earlier. Something on her face told him this was not a social call, and if wasn't a social call, that meant she had news to share, and there was only one kind of news he could think of that would be responsible for wiping the smile off a beautiful woman's face.

"Why do I have the feeling you're about to tell me something I'm not going to be too happy to hear?"

She motioned toward the bed, and he felt his mind start to detach from his body in the same way it did right before he climbed atop a bull. She stood there, her hair loose and long around her shoulder, a red T-shirt hugging her curves, plain jeans revealing the shape of her hips, and he knew, he just knew.

"I'm pregnant."

Good thing she'd told him to sit down.

Chapter Two

She hated blurting the news like that. Hated the way his face seemed to drain of color. Hated that she felt like some kind of lowlife for getting them into this predicament.

It takes two to tango.

She'd been repeating the words to herself the whole way to Southern California. It didn't help that she'd had to lie in order to escape the clutches of her family. They thought she'd flown west to talk to a potential sponsor, which meant she'd had to drag her publicity agent into the ordeal so that Amanda could cover for her. She hated asking Amanda to lie. Thank goodness the woman was professional enough not to ask questions.

"Are you sure?"

She almost laughed. "Oh, yes." She crossed her arms in front of herself. He hadn't seen the pregnancy tests lined up on her counter. "I'm sure."

He tipped his cowboy hat back, presumably so he could see her better, and she admitted the dark-haired cowboy was just as handsome as she had remembered with his sideburns and square chin. Pictures on the internet didn't do him justice. No wonder she'd fallen into bed with him.

"How?" He shook his head, the right side of his lips tipping up into a wry grin. "I mean, I know how, but you took precautions, right?"

"Of course I did." She placed her hands on her hips. "*You* were the one that didn't use a condom."

"I told you we should, but you were in such a dang hurry."

She took a deep breath because he was right. She'd been the one to tell him not to worry.

"I guess it doesn't really matter." She shook her head. "What's done is done, but in hindsight, it was a stupid mistake. My ob-gyn thinks I didn't take my birth control pills regularly enough—not," she quickly added, "that I missed any. I didn't. I just lead a busy life, and that weekend we were testing a new car and I wasn't on time and sometimes that can lead to trouble, or so I've learned the hard way."

His shoulders had tensed even more, she noticed. It was easy to spot given the breadth of them beneath his blue-checkered shirt.

"So what are you going to do?"

Okay, so points for not getting angry with her over the birth-control thing, or calling her names or reacting like a jerk. Negative points for using the word *you*.

"*We* are going to decide that together."

The shell-shocked look had begun to fade. He nodded, tipped his black cowboy hat back a bit more. A cowboy. That was so not her usual type, and yet here they were.

She turned, pulled up a chair and sat down across from him. The motel was a real dive. She had told herself not to feel insulted that he'd recommended it, but then she reasoned he'd been trying to keep their relationships under wraps and so had chosen a place off the beaten path. Still, the worn brown carpet and tiny little room wasn't exactly what she was used to when traveling. It smelled like an old jacket, and the brown bedspread looked worn. Their knees almost touched, and there was a window-mounted air conditioner next to them that'd clearly seen better days.

"You want to keep it?" he asked, his eyes wide and full of concern.

Did she want to keep it? She stared at her lap. His gaze seemed to see right through her and she didn't want him to glean that she'd considered terminating the pregnancy. It would be so simple. She wouldn't have to tell anyone. Just a quick trip to downtown Charlotte and she'd be done.

"I don't think I have a choice." She took a deep breath, looked into his eyes and felt the panic begin to subside. Something about his presence had that effect on her. She'd noticed it the night they'd met. He was like a balm to her souped-up soul. "I've always told myself if anything like this ever happened, I'd have the baby, not that I ever expected this to happen. But babies, they're a blessing, right? I refuse to just throw a life away." She shook her head, feeling close to tears again. "I can't. I just can't."

He nodded, and she really wanted to cry when she saw the understanding in his eyes. "But what about your career?"

And that was it. That was the reason she'd flown across the United States to see him. *What about it?* Decisions needed to be made, and she didn't want to make them alone. She needed to talk them out with someone, and who better than the baby's father?

"I would have to take a leave of absence." She felt her stomach flip again at the thought of breaking the news to her dad. "We'd have to find a substitute driver. I could still work for the team, help them out and what-not, but it'd have to be from the sidelines."

He was still nodding and, much to his credit, seemed to approve. "How do you think your family's going to take the news?"

She took a deep breath. "My dad's going to flip. My mom will support me. My brother Jarrod will never let me live it down, and neither will my younger brother and sister."

Her brother Jarrod raced cars, too. It was a family affair—her mom, dad, older brother and two younger siblings were all involved…would all be disappointed in her.

"And your fans? Your sponsor? Shouldn't you be concerned about that, too?"

He understood. Of course he would. He lived the life of a professional athlete, too. He was the one person in the world to whom she could confess all and, she hoped, help her to accept the grim truth: she was well and truly hosed.

"It'll be big scandal," she confessed. She went back to staring at her hands. "Our fan base is Southern, and you don't get pregnant out of wedlock in the South."

He leaned forward, prompting her to meet his gaze. He had a good soul. She could see it in his eyes. She'd known it that first night she'd met him, and her esti-mation of his character had only improved since see-ing him again. He could have no idea how much she appreciated his levelheaded assessment of the situation.

"Surely times have changed."

"Oh, they have, just not in the South. My sponsor's going to flip, too. I'm the pitch girl for MarriageMate. com. I guess people consider me sensible and trustworthy. I don't know how sensible they're going to think me once they discover I'm pregnant and the father is someone I barely know."

He leaned toward her and she thought for a moment he might stroke her cheek. "They don't have to know that," he said softly. "We could tell people we met months ago. That we've just kept it under wraps."

She'd thought about that, too. It would make things seem a little less tawdry.

His hand landed on her knee, his warm palm reassuring. "We could play it up. Say we're in love."

She held his gaze. "You mean lie."

The side of his mouth tipped into a half smile of chagrin. When he shrugged, she frowned because she hated the idea of lying to her fans. And what if some gossip rag decided to look into their so-called past? What if they discovered that her racing schedule and his rodeo schedule would have made a relationship next to impossible? Plus she was pretty sure it was obvious they'd never met before that night in Las Vegas. There'd been a very public introduction.

"I don't think that will work." She was about to remind him of their first meeting when her cell phone rang. She blanched when she saw who it was. Her mother. She hated having to fib to her mother.

"You need to get that?"

She nodded.

"Go on." He waved her away. "I'm not going anywhere."

He wouldn't, either. She'd worried during the whole

flight that he'd get upset. Blow up on her. Disappear. He hadn't and that reassured her more than anything. Everything would be all right, she told herself. She would just have to break the news to her family.

SHANE LISTENED TO Kaitlin's side of the conversation as he waited in her room. He didn't mean to eavesdrop. The walls were so thin he could hear a fly land on the sidewalk outside. He probably should have picked a better place for her to stay. He had a feeling the motel's clientele probably wasn't the best.

He was going to be a father. His stomach did the equivalent of being catapulted off a bull.

He leaned forward and rested his elbows on his knees. That didn't soothe his stomach. He scrubbed a hand over his face.

Daddy.

He couldn't imagine some little boy or little girl calling him that. And he realized in that instant that his life would be forever entwined with Kaitlin Cooper's. He couldn't imagine letting her raise a child alone, and for that reason he had a feeling she might agree to what he was about to suggest.

"Sorry about that," she said, her troubled eyes even more full of sadness and dismay when she came back into the room. "That was my mom checking up on me like she always does." She flicked her long hair over a shoulder.

He understood what that was like. His mom had been the same before she'd died during a surgery meant to save her life. They had more in common than they probably thought. One day, he'd tell her all about the remarkable woman who'd raised him.

"Look—" he took a deep breath "—I've been think-ing while you were on the phone."

She nodded, and he saw her sit up straighter, as if she expected bad news.

"I think we should get married."

Her shoulders went from rigid to slack. "What?"

"I think we should tell people the truth—that we met in Las Vegas. We could hedge a little about what happened afterward. We could say we've been seeing each other on the side ever since and that we fell in love and that we were going to hold off getting married, but you're pregnant and so we decided to make it official."

If he'd asked her to take her clothes off and jump off the Empire State Building, she couldn't have looked more shocked. "You want to marry me?"

No. Not really. He was just old-fashioned enough to want to marry a woman he loved. Someone he could settle down and grow old with. Marriage to a woman he barely knew was definitely *not* part of the game plan, and yet that was what he felt honor-bound to offer.

"Look. I've got sponsors, too. Even though it's not the same for a man as it is a woman—"

"So totally not fair."

He nodded in agreement. "I know, but it's still going to reflect poorly on me if your pregnancy gets any kind of media traction. Not saying it will. It's possible no-body will care. I mean, it's not like we're A-list stars, but the truth is, there's more to it than that."

Only as he said the words did he realize what was in his heart. It wasn't just to save face that he wanted to marry her.

"I want my kid to have my last name." His hands went slack in his lap as the tension drained from his body. "I know that sounds old school but I do. And I want him or her to know that I'm their daddy. No matter what happens between you and me, my kid is just that…my kid."

Her eyes had grown soft. He felt it then, that same little tickle in his belly that he'd felt the night he'd met her. It gave him pause, but only for a moment because she reached out and touched his knee and that had him feeling all kinds of different things.

"You're remarkable."

"You might not say that after you taste my cooking."

She smiled softly. "Are you sure?"

"About my cooking? Absolutely. My brother bought me a fire extinguisher for Christmas."

"No." She shook her head. "About getting married."

No. Not at all. He had a feeling this whole deal would end up a lot more complicated than he thought, but it was his fault, too. He should have worn protection that night. He hadn't.

So he nodded firmly. "I'm sure."

She drew back, stared at him for a long moment and then said, "All right, then. Marriage it is."

She still seemed pensive but less uncertain than she had earlier. He respected the hell out of her for not taking the easy way out. She hadn't flown to California and demanded marriage. She'd laid her cards out on the table and asked for his advice, and he respected her concerns, understood them, too. He might be scared to death, but he understood.

"Las Vegas?" he asked.

"Might as well. That's where it all started."

"We can drive there tonight if you want. Only a few hours away from here."

"Tonight?" Her brows had lifted.

"Why not?"

She considered his words. "Why not, indeed."

them, to the altar with its big stone cross and then back all over again…as if she sought silent reassurances from one of them.

"You look beautiful," he said when she reached his side.

The words caught her attention. She glanced down at herself.

"Do I? I'm afraid the girls at the department store went a little crazy when they heard I was getting married today. They insisted on going all out, bouncing me from department to department, and one of them was a race fan, and so she knew who I was and she helped me with the dress, even though I think it's way over the top. I thought about a veil, too, but I worried it'd be too much—"

"Kait."

She'd been about to take a breath, but he forestalled another gush of words with his hand. "It's okay."

He saw her eyes widen just before her lashes swept down. He saw her take a deep breath. Saw her hands clench the bouquet tighter. But when their gazes met again, there were tears in her eyes.

He gently squeezed her hand. "We're going to be fine."

She clung to him like a drowning sailor would a life raft. And it amazed him. Here was someone who drove two hundred miles per hour and who'd been in some horrific wrecks. Who routinely faced off with some of the toughest men in the racing industry but who feared her future to the point that her whole body trembled.

He squeezed her hand again. "Trust me. Things will work out."

He saw her take another breath and then she said, "Okay."

She seemed ready then, even took a step so that they were closer together. "You look great, too, you know."

Did he? He'd rented a tux from the wedding chapel, but he still wore his cowboy hat, and he hadn't taken the time to check his appearance to see how he looked. He'd been completely caught up in making all the arrangements while Kait went out to find a dress and get herself ready. It'd taken them hours to set things up. They'd started at the Las Vegas courthouse. Then they'd had to find a place that could actually marry them on such short notice. Then they'd had to wait because the chapel couldn't fit them in until early evening. He'd spent the time shopping for a wedding ring and then getting ready himself. He'd had no idea so many people would want to get married in Las Vegas, but it was hard not to feel like they were simply one couple in a long assembly line of future husbands and wives.

"Are we ready?" asked the Elvis look-alike.

"I guess so," she said.

The man nodded, opened his book. "Dearly beloved…"

SHE BARELY REMEMBERED the ceremony. Even now, as they signed the official marriage certificate, she couldn't recall the words the officiant had said.

"Congratulations," Natasha, the chapel's wedding coordinator, said. "You make such a beautiful couple."

What do you want to bet Natasha says that to everyone? Kait thought.

"If you head to the front of the chapel, our wedding photographer will meet you there to take pictures. They'll be beautiful this time of day."

Shane had insisted on the deluxe wedding package and she hadn't argued. At least they'd have pictures… and a ring on her finger. It caught the light as she set the pen down. She'd expected a plain gold band like the one she'd bought him. He'd gotten her a rock the size of a lug nut. Well, okay, maybe not that big, but it was tall and round and felt strange on her finger.

And so they went outside, the Vegas skyline already set aglow by the lights of the Strip, and posed in front of the Little Chapel on the Hill looking for all the world like a couple at a normal wedding. When they finished, she gathered her things and they both headed for Shane's red truck, which was easy to spot thanks to the rodeo logos and his sponsor's name painted across the doors.

"It's late," he said, glancing at the skyline. "And at some point I'll need to change out of this tux and return it, although I suppose I could do it right now before we leave."

"Maybe I should change out of my dress."

"No. Don't do that. It seems somehow…wrong. We should both stay in our wedding clothes."

He frowned and she could tell he was up to something. "What did you have in mind?"

"Well, it seems to me that we should have a wedding night." Then he quickly added, "Not that I expect anything, you know, physical. I just think we should spend the night here. Sort of make it seem more official. I think people will find it strange if we drive straight home tonight. Plus I don't fancy driving all the way back to Via Del Caballo with such a late start, and I'm pretty sure you're exhausted, too."

Tired didn't begin to describe the way she felt. Ever since she'd gotten pregnant, she'd been dragging herself around. Today was no exception.

"And hungry," she admitted. "Starving, actually."

He nodded. "I'll rent us a room. Unless you'd like to stay in your own room."

"No. That's okay. It might seem kind of strange to people if someone finds out you and I spent our wedding night in separate hotel rooms."

"That's my thinking, too, and I know just the place where we can stay."

Wherever they were headed, he didn't need to consult his GPS. He just drove straight to the hotel.

"Wow," she said when she spotted what looked like an Italian villa perched atop a small hill. The sign outside read Le Bellissime Ville.

"I've stayed here a few times over the years," he said as they crossed over a moat that ringed the perimeter of the place. Then they drove between a giant stone archway set into a three-story stucco facade that'd been backlit by a clever contractor. They entered a courtyard-style check-in area that so closely resembled an actual village that Kaitlin felt her mouth drop open.

"This is amazing," she said.

"I know. Crazy, isn't it?"

Multicolored buildings painted in beiges and browns and pinks stretched up around them. Each of them had a different level roofline, but all of the roofs were covered by something resembling wood shingles. The buildings differed in the type of windows and doorways set into their facade—some windows were square, some rounded, some with sashes, some without. Baskets of flowers hung between them, as did old-fashioned lanterns. The cobblestones continued so that it seemed as if they drove into the middle of a plaza.

"I like this place because it's private." He pulled beneath a porte cochere and stopped. "I'll go inside and book us a room."

"Do you need money?" she felt the need to ask.

"Don't be ridiculous." He smiled his million-dollar grin, the one that had won him bull-riding fans the world over. "You're my wife. What's yours is mine and what's mine is also mine."

It took her a second to glean his words but only because her attention had caught on the word *wife*. "Haha. Very funny."

But she had to force a smile.

Wife.

"I'll be right back," he said with a kind smile and a tip of his cowboy hat.

Left alone, she was struck by their situation again. Married. Pregnant. And her parents didn't even know.

Her stomach clenched, acid burning her insides. Food. She needed food because suddenly she felt sick.

It didn't take long for him to return but by the time he had, her panic had increased to the point that she felt light-headed.

"We're in luck. They had a suite available."

"Wasn't that expensive?"

He cocked a teasing brow. "I told you don't worry about it."

She nodded, but it made her woozy again. She touched her forehead, as if that might somehow help her brain from swimming.

"What's wrong?"

"Just a little dizzy is all."

And scared, all of a sudden. More frightened than even the first time she had climbed into a go-cart. She'd been five and scared to death, and then her dad had gently given her a shove and she'd taken off and that had been that. What she wouldn't give to have her dad here now.

She could feel tears creep into her eyes.

Shane turned toward an attendant and tossed him the keys. "Here," he said to the startled man wearing some kind of brocade jacket. "Park this for me. We're in the bridal suite."

He didn't wait for the man, well, the kid, really, to answer, he just darted around the front of his truck and pulled the door open. She felt like a complete ninny. She never cried. It wasn't allowed in racing. But ever since she'd gotten pregnant…

"Come here."

She stared at him, puzzled, not sure what he intended to do, and started to slip out of the truck.

He scooped her up in his arms. She gasped. He pulled her up against him.

"Shane, put me down."

"Not on your life," he said. "You're my wife and you're carrying my baby and you look like you're about to pass out."

"People are staring."

"So?"

But if people stared, it was only to smile when they spotted what no doubt appeared to be a happy couple that had just gotten married. She heard soft whispers of "How adorable" and more loudly called "Congratulations" and then someone saying "Hey. Isn't that Kaitlin Cooper?"

She hid her head in Shane's arms like she was ten years old, but it felt good to be tucked up against him. She wanted to close her eyes. To maybe go to sleep. To slip away into a dreamless world where she wasn't facing the prospect of motherhood and the end of her racing career. Well, the season at least.

Someone must have held the elevator door for them, because she heard them say, "What floor?"

"Five," Shane said.

"You can put me down now." She peeked a glance up at him.

"That's okay," he said, shifting a bit, and she realized they were alone as the doors closed. "You weigh next to nothing."

"I feel ridiculous."

"That's your inner race-car driver speaking. Hard to let go of control, I imagine. But you just stay right here. I'll set you down when we get to our room, then I'm ordering room service for a meal and you're going to relax and take it easy until you don't look as pale as that dress you're wearing, which is nice, by the way, but your cheeks shouldn't match the color of it."

Was she that pale? She felt like she'd been walloped by a pace car. It made her wonder if it was really the pregnancy or if something more was wrong with her.

The elevator dinged. And at the end of a long hallway was a room with a sign next to the door.

Bridal Suite.

"Hang on." She felt him shift her weight, his arm moving. How he managed to hold her and somehow find the card key was anybody's guess, but he did it.

The door emitted a beep, and he wasted no time using his butt to push it open. She gasped at the beauty of the room.

"Not bad, eh?"

It must have cost him a small fortune. She had expected quaint and cozy. They'd gotten lavish and extravagant. Off-white marble floors covered a space nearly as large as her home back in North Carolina. In the middle sat a sunken conversation pit surrounded by marble columns. A dining area was to their left, and to their right she caught a glimpse of the bedroom. He took her straight to the sunken living room, or whatever one would call it, the scent of a massive bouquet of flowers reminding her of the honeysuckle that grew outside her home. It made her instantly homesick.

"Don't move," he said after depositing her on a plush off-white couch. From beyond an arched window, she could spy the entire Las Vegas Strip. It stood as yet another reminder that she was far from home.

"Here." He handed her a bottled water. "Drink this." He even opened it for her, and as she looked into his blue eyes she found herself thinking that she'd gotten lucky with him. He could have completely brushed her off, in more ways than one, and yet here he was treating her like fine china, and it was…nice.

Oh, no. Don't you be going down that road.

That was all she needed, to develop feelings for him. They were having a baby together. That was all. He had married her out of kindness. When this was all over and done with, she'd go back to her life in North Carolina and he'd go back to his.

Right?

Chapter Four

Shane had never, not ever, seen a woman eat like Kait had, then pass out on a couch so fast. He might have thought something was wrong with her if he hadn't called a bull-riding friend with five kids. He'd reassured Shane that pregnant women were notorious for gulping down food and instantly falling asleep, but then the friend had asked who was pregnant. Shane had hung up on him.

Snnnnnnnkkkkk.

He looked over at the couch from where he was sitting at the dining table, the remains of their dinner still in front of him, and saw the tiny body emitting a sound unlike any he'd never heard before.

Snnnnnnnnnnn.

Snoring.

Yup, he thought, crossing the room. *Definitely her.* The product of a million masculine fantasies, and there she was, mouth wide open, head cocked back, hair falling off her head. A part of him wondered what her fans would say if they could see her now. It made him smile, and he scooted in closer, taking care his cowboy boots were nothing more than a gentle shuffle on the marble steps that led to the sunken seating area. She still wore her wedding dress. Still had little sparkly things in her hair. That couldn't be comfortable. The thing was as tight as snakeskin, and yet you couldn't tell she was pregnant.

She was carrying his baby and that should scare the piss and vinegar out of him, but it didn't. He should probably wake her up, though, and maybe ask if she wanted to change, although now that he thought about it, they hadn't exactly planned for an overnighter. Did she have extra clothes? Where were the ones she'd been wearing before she'd arrived at the church? He'd shed his jacket the moment they'd ordered dinner, his sleeves were rolled up and his cowboy hat was sitting on the peg of a chair.

The sound of her snores grew even more pronounced. Her elegant hairstyle had started to come undone. But she looked adorable lying there and so at peace. He hated to disturb her.

"Kait," he said softly. "Wake up."

She didn't move.

"Kait, honey."

Another snore. And just for a moment he'd thought about what it would be like if this were a real wedding and what she would have done if he'd reached down and gently kissed her cheek. Only this wasn't real. And he couldn't kiss her and it frustrated the hell out of him.

Not meant to be, buddy.

He needed to move her, though. She'd roll off that couch. Plus that dress really didn't look comfortable, so for the second time that day, he found himself slipping his arms beneath her. She hardly stirred, just tipped her head into the crook of his arm and everything inside him stilled and he just stared down at her in wonder. How had he, a bull rider, ended up holding Kaitlin Cooper, star of stock-car racing? He would bet he was one of the few men in the world who knew she snored.

The bedroom was just as lavish as the rest of the bridal suite. Off-white coverlet. Marble floors. Ivory window curtains. Beyond a massive double door, there appeared to be a terrace with hanging plants and yet more flowers, and it was good to focus his attention on the room because it kept his mind off other things, like how her breasts seemed ready to escape the confines of her dress.

"Kait," he said again as he gently laid her down.

She was out. If she'd been a prizefighter, the referee would be at the ten count. But now that he'd thought about it, she'd had a busy twenty-four hours. She'd left early to meet him in Via Del Caballo. He'd swept her into his car not long after and driven her to Vegas. She'd spent the rest of the day getting ready for their wedding. No wonder she slept so soundly.

He slowly slipped his arms out from beneath her and stood above her.

She was his *wife*.

If the circumstances were different, he would have been proud to call her that on this day. But he wasn't proud. He was embarrassed. He shouldn't have gotten her in this situation in the first place, but, damn, she was beautiful. He took a moment to admire her. Even with her blond hair all topsy-turvy and her generous mouth open, she did it for him. She had sweeping brows that arched above widely spaced eyes. She had a tiny frame but voluptuous curves. That body was usually covered by a firesuit, one that concealed her figure, but her wedding dress revealed every glorious inch of her, and it was strewn with crystals that caught the light and made her seem like some kind of ethereal being. She probably wouldn't even feel him kiss her.

In theory.

He knew it had been a bad idea to give in to impulse because clearly Kait was like Snow White. One slight brush of his lips and her eyes popped open.

He froze. She blinked. He drew back. She smiled. He leaned in and kissed her again, this time on the lips. She seemed to melt back into the bed, and it wasn't what he'd expected her to do, but he didn't give it much thought because, like the first time he'd kissed her, his whole world shifted. The room faded away and it was just the warmth of her mouth and then the taste of her, which somehow, crazily, reminded him of strawberries. He would never remember lifting his hand and cupping the side of her face, but he must have done so because she tipped toward him, changing the angle of their mouths, and then her tongue found his own and he heard himself groan.

Crazy.

It was like standing on a firecracker, and the explosion reverberated through his body. She moaned, too, and then pulled back.

"We shouldn't."

Her eyes were huge and luminous, and he could see uncertainty in them along with surprise and something else, something that looked an awful lot like desire.

"It's our wedding night."

He sounded like an idiot, or like some guy just saying whatever to get the girl.

"It's not like that with us."

He knew what she meant, he'd had the same thought,

and yet he found himself leaning down so that they were nearly nose to nose and he realized she smelled like strawberries, too.

"Does is really matter?"

He still held her cheek, his thumb brushing the softness of her jaw. Up close, her eyes looked even bigger, her skin even more flawless, her lips teasing him with their nearness.

"I guess not."

She blinked, didn't move, and he realized it was up to him to make the choice. It was hell staring down at her and knowing he could have her when what he should really do was get up and walk away. Yet he wanted her with such a fierceness it was all he could do to keep his heart in his chest.

"You're right. We shouldn't."

He started to stand, but her hand caught his and his eyes found hers, and he knew that she'd ended up making the choice instead. He needed no second prompting, and he bent down and kissed her again and this time it was like riding a wild horse, one that bolted from the gate, and all he could do was hang on.

She shifted beneath him and he realized the pearls of her wedding dress pressed into his borrowed shirt and that seemed like a perfectly good reason to get rid of said dress. He didn't think twice, and she didn't, either, because her own fingers were busy undoing buttons, but the dang dress wouldn't come undone.

She broke off the kiss. "It has a hook." Her eyes were big and soft, and it seemed impossible to reconcile the sexy kitten staring up at him with the woman who'd been sawing some z's earlier.

"Here." She sat up, the dress hugging her curves as

she turned her back to him. He couldn't help himself.
He bent and kissed her bare shoulder, and if he was honest with himself, he'd been wanting to do that since the
moment he'd spotted her at the end of the aisle. He'd
never seen a woman more beautiful in his life.

And she's mine.

The possessiveness of his thoughts gave him pause.

But then he forgot everything as the taste of her lin-
gered on his lips and the smell of her made him close
his eyes, his mouth moving up the column of her neck.

She leaned into him, tipped her head sideways. He
buried his fingers in her hair, finding and then remov-
ing the clips or pins or whatever she'd used to hold it
aloft. It came tumbling down a moment later. Her dress
slid down her torso, and he knew this would be the
world's fastest seduction because he trembled. Damn,
she did it for him.

She turned again, lay back down, and he bent and
kissed a rosy-pink nipple. Her hips lifted and he realized
she was trying to shimmy out of her dress. He reached
down and helped her, gently suckling her flesh, bringing back memories of their first night in Vegas. He'd
been completely unable to control himself then, too.
They'd gone to her hotel room, but they'd barely made
it to the door before they'd started kissing.

"Shane." His name was a mere whisper, but the
sound of it on her lips did something else to him, too.

The dress fell away. His hand brushed something on
her thigh. A garter belt.

He met her gaze. "They went all out, didn't they?"

She was panting. "They did."

"Should I take it off with my teeth?"

Her stomach moved—a huff of laughter, he realized.

"Do whatever you want."

His whole body stilled. Whatever he wanted? Oh, he could think of a few things to do.

His fingers found the edge of the elastic, sliding it down, and though that was all he did—touch her—those blue eyes of hers went wide and her breathing grew more pronounced. He didn't even remember slipping off his shirt, but it was on the floor. She wore gauzy panty hose, too, the thigh-high kind, and the sight of her lying there in nothing but sexy lingerie made him groan and then dip his head, his lips following the path of the garter he tugged from her leg.

It was torture to move so slowly, but he wanted to savor each moment. He gently removed the flimsy material, and each time he kissed and caressed her legs, goose bumps appearing on her flesh, until at last she was naked. He sat back. Her eyes had grown dark. Her rib cage, so small and delicate looking, and yet filled with a massively courageous heart, rose and fell. Beautiful. A part of him wondered how he could be so lucky.

"Kiss me," she said.

He did as asked, his lips landing atop her thigh. She lifted her hips. He shifted upward ever so slightly, another kiss landing slightly above the first. She wiggled. He continued his trek upward and he knew he drove her nuts. When he nipped her belly, she groaned. When he suckled her nipple again, she arched against him. When he bit the side of her neck, she fumbled for the catch of his pants.

"No," he said, drawing back, his hand skating down her side. "Let's take it slow."

Her eyes widened ever so slightly and he studied

her flushed cheeks and her tousled hair as he wondered why he felt like he walked a high wire. As if everything were centered on a tiny line and he didn't want to make the wrong move because if he did, it might all be over. Such a strange thought to have, he admitted, kissing her again.

Her hand found him. He gasped, and she thrust her tongue into his mouth, taking charge of the situation and driving him closer to the edge. He told himself to pull back, but he couldn't seem to manage it. He kept kissing her and thinking to himself that he'd never met a woman who tasted so perfect.

She undid his pants. He let her unzip him even though he knew she'd bring him nearer to completely losing control. A part of him shouldn't be surprised. She was a woman known for her aggression on the track. Of course she would want to take charge in the bedroom, too. And still he didn't want it to be fast and furious, so he jerked away from her touch when she parted his pants.

"Not yet," he whispered.

"Yes," she hissed back, rubbing her foot against his calf.

"No." And before she could say another word, he shifted down, back to her nipples, his mouth capturing her, his hand finding the center of her. She gasped, tried to touch him again, but he wouldn't let her, just kept kissing and touching her. Her hips lifted, following the motion of his hand, and he slipped to the side of her and watched the play of emotions as she climbed higher and higher. This was what he wanted—to please her. To watch as she lost control.

She cried out. He kissed her again, his whole body tight with pent-up longing. He could feel her rush of pleasure, knew the exact moment she fell over the edge, and all he wanted to do was kiss her and hold her as she gently floated back to earth.

Chapter Five

"No fair," she told him, touching his cheek, relishing the feel of the stubble on his face.

He smiled down at her. "We have all night."

She didn't want to think about that. Didn't want to admit to herself that spending the night in his bed was probably a bad idea. Didn't want to do anything but bring him to his knees like he'd just done to her, so she quickly straddled him before he had time to do more than gasp.

"Your turn."

He shook his head.

She took the choice away from him, sliding down and finding him and taking him before he could stop her.

"Kait."

And she triumphed at the sound of his voice and the way his eyes closed, and he tipped his head back and hissed in pleasure. Now he would know how she felt. What it was like to lose control so quickly and completely that it blew her mind and made her wonder what it was about the man that touched her so deeply.

His neck drew her downward, and Kait kissed him and thought he tasted better than any dessert she'd ever had. When she nipped his ear, she felt his whole body tense and then flex and she knew he drew closer to losing control. Her own body still shuddered and, to her surprise, it began to build again—the coils of satisfaction seemed to pierce her soul. She stopped thinking then, lost herself to the spirals of pleasure that let her climb higher and higher until they both cried out. Exhausted, Kait rested her head against his chest.

"You're something else."

His voice rumbled against her ear, mixing with the beats of his heart, and she smiled because she knew how he felt, but then her smile faded. They shouldn't have been intimate again. She didn't need to develop feelings for him. This was a business deal. And when the baby came, there'd be even more stress on the two of them. Still, she couldn't seem to stop herself from kissing him on the chest before rolling off of him. He pulled her close. She thought about pulling away, but she was so tired…

She should really sleep on the couch. Things would be so much simpler if she kept him at arm's length.

So much simpler…

It was her last thought before she drifted off into a dreamless sleep.

She woke to the sound of her cell phone ringing. It shot her out of bed so fast she saw spots for a second, but a quick glance at a sleeping Shane revealed how soundly he slept.

She snatched a sheet from the bed, which she knew was odd given how intimate they'd been that night, and followed her ears to the location of her phone.

Her mom.

She should have known she'd call. Sarah Cooper had been dubious of her mysterious trip to the West Coast. Kait had seen it in her mom's eyes.

"Hi, Mom."

Her heart pounded because her mom had a way of knowing when she was up to no good. It was entirely possible someone had spotted her in Vegas and her mom had found out.

"Hi, sweetie. Just checking to see how your meeting went."

Kait's spine lost some of its rigidity. She clutched her phone a little closer, trying to project a tone of normalcy into her voice. "It went fine."

She hated lying, just hated it, and she hoped like heck her mom didn't ask her any more questions.

"You sound upset about it."

The sound of her mom's concern filled her with even more guilt. A girl couldn't ask for a better mother than Sarah Cooper. Her mom was her best friend. She told her everything. Except this. She'd kept the biggest news in her life from one of the few people on earth who had her back since forever, and it killed her to do so.

She was pregnant. She was married. And her mother didn't know a thing about it.

"Mom," she said softly, tentatively.

Her mom didn't push, and that was just like her, too, even though Kait was sure her mother knew something was wrong. Still, she couldn't get the words out.

"Honey, what is it?"

She sank down on the couch debating how much to tell her, but it was like a boil. She needed to lance it, but damned if she knew how.

"Mom, I'm…" Her fingernails gripped the hard plastic of her cell phone. "Mom, I'm pregnant."

Silence. She could hear the echo of her heartbeat through the handset. And then…laughter, which was absolutely not what she was expecting.

"Ha, ha, ha," her mom teased. "Very funny."

This was it. The moment of truth. She could play it off as a joke, too, save her news for later. Or she could let the truth come out.

"I wasn't kidding," she said firmly, seriously and with utter sincerity so that her mom knew she wasn't kidding.

Sarah Cooper went quiet again but only for a second. "Oh, honey."

There was shock in her mom's voice and disbelief and, God help her, a tinge of disappointment.

"Is that why you're in California?" she asked. "Is the father there?"

"He is."

"I knew it. I knew something was wrong. I could tell when you stopped by the shop."

I'm married, too.

The words were on the tip of her tongue. But that little tidbit of information she would save for later. She'd let the news of her pregnancy sink in first. Her mom would probably have a heart attack if she learned she was married, too.

"What does the father say?"

This, at least, was a point she could make in her favor. "He supports me one hundred percent." She took a deep breath. "You'll like him, Mom. He's a super nice guy. And he treats me right."

Kait could hear her mother breathing now. She was

probably standing in her spacious kitchen, more than likely barely hanging onto the phone. Kait could picture her standing there, and for a moment homesickness overcame her to the point that she felt close to crying.

"When will we get to meet him?"

Kait caught movement out of the corner of her eye. Shane stood at the entrance to the bedroom dressed in his boxers and a white T-shirt, but at least he wasn't naked. She swore her cheeks heated up with him standing there, as if her mom could see him through the phone somehow.

"Soon." She took her own deep breath. "I'll talk to you later, Mom."

"Kait, wait—"

She froze but didn't hang up. Her mom took her time framing words.

"I'm not going to pretend I'm happy about this. It's going to lead to a lot of…complications."

What an understatement.

"But I hope you know I love you and support you no matter what."

She swallowed. Hard.

"And you could have told me about this before you left."

She could have, but she'd wanted to see Shane first to know if he'd be there for her, because as crazy as it sounded, she wanted her parents to have a good opinion of him. Maybe they'd think better of her and her stupid mistake if they knew she didn't have poor choice in men, too.

"I know, Mom. I understand."

She hung up before her mom could say another word.

Shane stood there staring at her, and she knew he'd overheard.

"What did she say?"

The concern on his face nearly undid her. Damn the way her eyes kept wanting to sprout leaks. She really wished he hadn't overheard all that.

"She said she wished I would have told her."

He took a step forward, and she tried not to feel self-conscious, as if she didn't know him well enough to be near him half dressed, but that seemed ridiculous given what they'd done last night.

"Why didn't you?" he asked, taking a seat next to her.

This morning his five o'clock shadow looked more like a 10:00 p.m. blackout. The darkness of his razor stubble seemed to accentuate his sideburns and the thickness of his lashes. He could have been a character in a movie right then. The handsome hero come to soothe the troubled heroine. The backdrop of the pristine hotel room with its early morning sunlight and marble floors only lent itself to the fantasy.

"I think because I was ashamed."

He reached for her hand. She told herself not to move but found herself squeezing his hand back.

"We're going to get through this," he said. "You'll see." And then something flickered in his eyes, something that made him pull his hand back and stand up. "First step, though, is getting back to Via Del Caballo before nightfall and breaking the news to my family."

Her stomach dropped at the thought of it. What if they didn't like her? What if they tried to convince them to abort the baby? She could never do that. What if *she* didn't like *them*?

She hugged her stomach.

"You feeling okay?"

She swallowed back bile. "I just need to eat."

It was all happening too fast. Too many changes. And now her mom knew, and Kait would bet her mom would tell her dad, especially since Kait hadn't asked her mom to keep the news to herself.

"Why don't I order breakfast? You sit here and relax."

He was worried about the baby. She could see it in his eyes. She forced herself to relax, pressed a hand on her belly and told the child there that everything would be okay. And it would be okay. She needed to pick herself up and look to the future.

"Thanks."

For being there for her. For not making her feel like a complete loser. For helping her to forget last night, even if it was only for a few hours, that her life was in complete chaos. He would be a good father. She didn't know how she knew that, but she did.

It's too bad they would never have a real marriage.

Chapter Six

By the time they made it back to Gillian Ranch, the sun was high in the sky, painting the fields around the ranch a shade of green Kait had never seen before. In North Carolina the grass was dark. Here it was more yellow. As if the sun shone from inside of it.

"This is it," Shane said as they crossed beneath a metal sign with a *G* and a sideways *R* on it. "Home sweet home."

Acres and acres of rolling green hills dotted by massive valley oaks with thick shadows beneath them lay behind a rock wall that seemed to stretch as far as the eye could see.

"Good gracious. How much land does your family own?"

Shane shot her a sideways look beneath his straw cowboy hat. "Between my dad and uncle?" He frowned in thought. "I think it's about thousand acres, more or less. Each family has five hundred acres to manage."

She felt her jaw go slack. She had no idea why she'd thought Shane's family were... She had to think for a moment because exactly what *had* she thought? That they were poor? She'd known he was at the top of his game and that he must make decent money, but this was a whole different level than what she'd thought.

"It's impressive."

On either side of the road was a rock wall that must double as a fence. Beyond it, on either side, were acres of grassland studded with oak trees. She could see cattle grazing in the distance.

"My dad and uncle bought the land when it was pretty inexpensive."

She had a feeling even back then it probably hadn't been cheap. "Who built that wall?"

"Old Spanish settlers. It crosses and crisscrosses our property. Part of some kind of land grant ages ago."

Her perception of him underwent a shift. She'd had this idea in his head that he came from a poor, country family. Clearly that wasn't the case at all…

"Your dad used to rodeo." That much she remembered from her quick search of the internet.

"Both my dad and uncle did. That's how they were able to buy this place. They pooled their purse money together and bought the place, oh, thirty or so years ago. Before my dad met my mom. Turned out to be a smart decision. This is all my dad and uncle's land. I have the option to buy some land from them, but I'm not there yet. My dad is pretty firm that we all need to earn our own way in the world."

"They must have been really, really good at what they did," she muttered as they wound their way through low-lying hills.

"Ten time world champions between the two of them."

How had she not known this? Her Google search had mentioned his dad was famous in the rodeo world and that he'd won world championships, but this went beyond that. It was like finding out a big-league pitcher had been to the World Series not once but several times. Unbelievable.

"What's your mom like?"

His face froze. His hand tightened on the steering wheel. Emotions flitted across his face. All this she saw and more in just a brief flicker until he closed the shutters of his eyes.

"She died a few years back."

And it'd hit him hard. "I'm so sorry."

He took a deep breath. "The rest of my family is alive and well. You'll meet them all today."

"All?"

"It's Sunday. Family dinner night. We switch back and forth between ranches, but tonight's my dad's turn."

Wait. Just how many houses were on the Gillian property?

And then she saw the family homestead and what a view it was—like something out of a travel guide.

The hills had parted and up ahead sat a low-lying valley with a vineyard stretching to the north and south and a road intersecting the middle of it. And just past that, some kind of massive barn with a terra-cotta roof. And beyond that, a home up on small hill that was the same color as the cotton-candy clouds above, off-white, with a veranda that ran along the back side. She spotted a second home then, one just as large as the first but a little ways away on a different hilltop.

"Just how wealthy *is* your family?"

It seemed impertinent to ask, but the sight of the massive estate and all the outbuildings took her aback.

She'd pictured something so entirely different that she couldn't quite wrap her mind around it all.

"I don't know, actually." He looked over at her as they started to drive through the vineyards. "My dad doesn't share that kind of information. He believes we all need to make our own way in the world. But I know my dad and uncle were smart with their money. The vineyard might be on the smaller scale compared with some, but they were one of the first to plant vines in this area and now there's a whole host of vineyards trying to buy up land here. Plus there's the cattle operation. And the cutting horses. So I'm guessing my dad and uncle do okay."

They'd started up the small hill, driving on an asphalt strip with a slight drop-off on either side, and as they rounded a small turn to the right, the view took her breath away. Or maybe that was nerves. She could see cars and trucks parked at all angles in front of a gorgeous Spanish-style house that seemed to stretch on forever.

"Looks like everyone's here."

She drove race cars for a living. She'd met some of the most powerful and influential people over the years. She'd even jumped out of a plane once upon a time. Nothing had prepared her for the fear she felt upon facing the prospect of meeting Shane's family.

"Do they have any idea about us?"

He parked the truck, turned to look at her, and he was back, the man who stared at her with kindness and consideration and made her heart beat in a whole other way. She didn't know why this California cowboy with his starched jeans and straw hat made her melt in her seat, but he did.

"They don't but you have nothing to worry about." He patted her leg. "Our family's known for doing crazy and unconventional stuff."

He slipped out of the truck. She prepared to do the same, but he intercepted her after she opened the door and held it for her like some kind of gallant knight of old. And when he took her hand to help steady her as she slid off the high seat, she found herself wanting to hold on to those big fingers of his, but she couldn't do that.

Business deal, remember?

Sooner or later she'd return to North Carolina, at least for a little bit. She shouldn't get used to depending on him or having him around.

"Ready?"

No. "Let's go."

She could do this. It was just like a meet and greet at the racetrack. She'd always been good at those. She'd learned from an early age how to pour on the Cooper charm. Except her last name was no longer Cooper.

Her palms were sweating. She'd chosen jeans and a red shirt that hugged her curves but didn't show off too much, thanks to a boatneck collar. But the coolness of her outfit did nothing to allay the heat of her cheeks as she entered the house. Terra-cotta tiles led the way to an open seating area framed by thick beams and a high ceiling. Off to her left, just inside the door, hung framed numbers, each of them with *NFR* across the top. At least ten of them. Souvenirs from the national finals, she realized, a few of them with Shane's name on the bottom.

Outside, she could hear the sound of voices on the veranda. Someone laughed. The sound of ice in glasses. The smell of roses someone had placed on a nearby side table. These were the things she would remember for the rest of her life.

Shane walked ahead of her. She didn't mean to, but she hung back a bit. Okay, so she freaked out and stopped well back from the ornate double doors with Spanish-style scrollwork embedded into the glass. The home would do some of her racing friends proud.

"Hey, hey!" someone, a male someone with thick sweeping brows and a dented chin, said. "Look who's here."

"You made it back," said someone else, a stunning woman with black hair and the same thick lashes as the men in her family. Kait wondered if she was a sister or a cousin. So many people sat around a large table it was hard to take them all in and it made her feel even more intimidated, but so far nobody had spotted her hiding behind the veranda doors.

"I told you I would," Shane said. He turned and she saw him jerk in surprise when he realized she wasn't right behind him. His eyes connected with her own. She froze. He motioned with his hands.

"Uh-oh," said the first man, and Kait realized she'd been spotted. "Who's this?"

And it was time. No escaping it. The moment had come.

Taking a deep breath, she tentatively moved forward. Shane turned back to his family.

"Everyone, this is my wife."

You could have heard a pin drop.

Shane looked around the table and tried not to wince. Of course it was his brother Carson who laughed. He leaned back in the heavy wooden chair that matched the ancient oak table his family, including his aunt and uncle and cousins, sat around and guffawed. Jayden, his sister, was in the midst of setting down a tray of olives she'd just pilfered from, her hand frozen in midair, and she looked anything but amused. And his father, well, Shane refused to look at his father.

"That's funny," Carson said when he stopped chuckling. He looked around the table, clearly wanting to share in the joke with everyone else. But nobody said a word, probably because it wasn't in Shane's nature to joke around, and his family knew it.

Shane glanced at Kait. She tried to smile, but it was rocky at best.

"Hey," said his cousin Tyler. "Isn't that Kaitlin Cooper?"

Leave it to his cousin to recognize Kait's famous face.

"Did he say wife?" his aunt Crystal asked.

"I think he did," said Uncle Bob.

"Hey, everyone," Kait said during a slice of silence. She waved.

"Wait," Carson said. "Are you for real?"

His little brother's eyes grew wide, and given his prominent eyebrows, the look seemed exaggerated. He pulled his gaze away from Kait to stare around the table.

"We were married yesterday," Shane announced, pulling Kait to his side. He held up his hand just in case they thought he was still joking. Kait followed suit, showing them her ring finger, and it must have been the sight of the diamond he'd bought her that convinced his family because suddenly everyone was speaking at once. His sister was the first person to stand up, rushing around the table to greet Kait.

"Congratulations," she said. She leaned in and gave Kait a hug, and Shane could tell Kait was surprised by the greeting.

"You are Kaitlin Cooper," said his cousin. "Right?"

She forced the wattage of her smile up a notch. "I am."

"Wow." Carson seemed genuinely impressed. "How'd you bag her?"

"Carson," he chastised. Leave it to his brother to say something like that. The man didn't have a serious bone in his body. "She's standing right here."

"It's okay." Kait turned her smile up to its full effect. "I can take it."

He would bet she could. She drove cars at two-hundred-plus miles per hour. It was so easy to forget these days. He'd gotten to know the woman, not the race-car driver.

"So your father is Lance Cooper?" This from his other cousin, Levi, a carbon copy of his uncle Bob right down to the green eyes.

"He is."

"Wow." He tipped his cowboy hat back, peering up at her with an expression as close to awe as he'd ever seen on his cousin's face.

And still not a word from his dad, who sat at the end of the massive table like a disapproving sovereign. He even resembled one with his bushy gray brows, somewhat longer hair that matched his brows and his patrician nose. That was what he'd heard his mom call it once upon a time.

"I don't care who she is," said Aunt Crystal, standing up and coming around the table. "She's cute as a button and part of the family now."

He could always count on Crystal to make someone feel at home. When his mom had died, it was his aunt who'd gotten him through the dark moments. He should have figured she would welcome his new wife with open arms.

Wife. It still took some getting used to.

"You want to sit down?" Crystal asked. She turned back to the table. "Dylan, move on down a seat."

Everyone shuffled around, and Shane risked another glance at his father. He was busy eating whatever appetizer came before the meat Shane could smell roasting on the barbecue. He didn't look up and it might have been that his face was in shadow thanks to the thick beams overhead, but his expression seemed dark. He could see his uncle Bob peeking glances, and Bob frowned at what he saw. As luck would have it, room was made so Shane could sit right next to his father.

"Dad," he said before he sat down.

His dad grunted. His beige shirt matched his straw cowboy hat. He didn't look up.

Damn him.

Kait took a seat next to Shane. He waited for his father to look up and finally acknowledge her. Kait clearly knew something wasn't right with the eldest Cooper because she stared at him, puzzled.

"Dad, this is Kait."

His dad finally met his gaze, and Shane almost flinched. There was so much disappointment deep in his eyes that it took him aback. He knew why, too, and it had everything to do with the three Ps of success, at least according to his dad. Perseverance. Passion. Purpose.

None of that will mean a hill of beans if you let a girl turn your head.

How many times had he heard the lecture? So he knew why his dad sat there fuming. It'd always been Reese Gillian's dream to have his son follow in his footsteps. He wanted him to continue the Gillian rodeo legacy of winning as many NFR titles as he could. And he had, to some degree, succeeded. But it wasn't enough. Nothing was ever enough for his dad.

Reese Gillian set his fork down. "Is she pregnant?"

The words had been dropped into one of those odd moments of silence where everyone seemed to stop talking at once. He saw his aunt flinch. His brother Cooper looked in his direction, probably trying to gauge his reaction. In fact, half the table seemed to lean in a little and then draw back.

Something snapped inside him then. Something that'd been rolling and boiling and bubbling to the surface from the moment he'd walked out into the patio and been ignored.

He took off his hat and soothed his hair before cramming it back on again. His hands shook. "She's my *wife*, Dad." He glared at his father. "What difference does it make?"

His dad leaned forward. "Is she?"

"Yes."

Someone moved. It was Kait. "Excuse me." She threw a napkin someone must have handed her back on the table and ran off before he could call her back.

Chapter Seven

She'd never been more humiliated in her life.

The house seemed to swallow her up, and she was grateful for that. Out on the veranda, the sudden eruption of voices made it seem as if her leaving had popped the cork on a bottle of good behavior. There were raised voices and accusations, and she just wanted to get away from them. She reached for the front door.

"Kait."

A hand fell on her own. She hadn't even heard Shane follow her into the house. She'd been too blinded by her own tears.

Tears.

Damn her stupid hormones. She hated how sensitive she'd gotten.

"Don't leave."

He wedged himself in front of her, and she froze because when she looked into his eyes she saw misery there and it took her by surprise. Her hand slipped away from the door.

"That was rude. And—" he blinked and she lost sight of his eyes behind the brim of his cowboy hat for a moment "—uncalled-for. I should have waited for the right time to break our news. We should have done it together."

His apology smothered the flames of her anger, but she still couldn't imagine going back out there again. When she heard the back door slide open, he must have seen the panic in her eyes.

"Come here."

He didn't give her time to answer, just grabbed her hand and led her down a hall with heavy wooden doors on the right and a wall of windows to the left. Their feet made hardly a sound on the terra-cotta floor.

"In here."

She smelled it first. Him. His smell. How strange that she should know it so well already. She knew the moment she entered the room that it'd been his in the past. His childhood room, though it had long since been stripped of almost all things Shane. A few items remained. A picture of him atop a chest of drawers to her left. An old rope hanging around the bedpost to her right. And above the bed, belt buckles. Dozens of them but behind glass in a shadow box that reflected the light that came through windows overlooking the back of the house. On them she could make out the word "champion" above the silhouette of a bull. Beneath that were dates. He must have won them all when he was a kid.

"Sit," he ordered.

She didn't like being ordered around, not usually, but today she surrendered to his bossiness mostly because she was exhausted. Pregnancy seemed to be kicking her butt.

She sat.

"Look. My dad and I are…" He sank onto the bed

next to her and swiped a hand across his face. "We don't exactly see eye to eye sometimes."

"I can tell."

Along the short wall that held the door stood another dresser, this one lower and with a picture of Shane in front of a rodeo-announcer's booth, or so she guessed. He held a buckle, and next to him stood his dad and what must be his mother. But while his dad stood by his side, it was his mother who had her arm around him and who smiled proudly into the camera. She realized where Shane got his good looks from. Mrs. Cooper—gosh, she didn't even know her name—but Mrs. Cooper reminded her of a movie-star cowgirl, one with perfectly coiffed blond hair, a trim figure and a smile that had probably won her the title of rodeo queen.

"He just gets under my skin." He shook his head, looked into her eyes again. "But that's no excuse for blurting our news like that."

She released a huff of exasperation. "At least it's out in the open now."

He nodded. "There is that."

But then she looked down at her hand, at the diamond that sparkled on her ring finger. It was beautiful, far prettier than she had expected or maybe even deserved given the situation they were in.

"Where will we live?"

The question had been burning a hole in her brain for hours. She'd been afraid to ask. So many uncertainties and unknowns. She hadn't wanted to open the flood-gates of problem solving. Now seemed like as good a time as ever.

"Here, I guess. In Via Del Caballo."

"Shane, I have a life in North Carolina."

"I know, but my horses are here."

"And my race cars are back east."

"But you won't be racing."

The reminder smacked her in the face. She stared at her hands again.

"I'll need to return home to help my family find a replacement for me."

"I know. But it will seem strange if you stay there too long."

He was right. They would need to keep up appearances. "Come with me."

"Unfortunately, I have horses I need to keep maintained because bull riding isn't my only rodeo event, it's just the one I'm really good at. And then there's my job here at the ranch, but we can get to that in a minute. For now, I think you should stay here. At least in the beginning."

He had a point. "Okay, fine." She took a deep breath. "I think we should also work out some of the other details."

"You mean other than telling people we eloped and I knocked you up?"

He smiled, and it was the kindness in his eyes that made her think she could have done far worse when it came to picking a father to her baby.

Her stomach dropped again at the thought of their baby growing inside her.

Sooner or later she'd get used to the idea, but for now, she needed to focus. "Daytona is in a couple weeks and my family will need my help, especially now that I'm leaving them in the lurch. Hopefully, my mom will have broken the news to my dad that I'm pregnant and he'll have started searching for a replacement driver."

Her phone hadn't blown up, so she kind of doubted her mom had spilled the beans yet.

Chicken. You should have told him.

But she just couldn't do it. She wouldn't be able to stomach the disappointment in his eyes. And that was something, at least, she and Shane shared—they both had fathers that were an integral part of their careers.

"How about I fly home for few days and then come back next weekend?"

He nodded. "I could fly to North Carolina with you the following week. That would give me time to find someone to take over my ranch duties."

"You could meet my parents."

He winced. "What fun."

It was her turn to smile reassuringly. "They're not that bad." Probably less intimidating than his family.

As if she'd summoned them with her thoughts, someone knocked on Shane's bedroom door.

"You guys decent?" It was his aunt Crystal. "Can I come in?"

Shane leapt up from the bed and opened the door.

"Well," she said, placing her hand on her hips. "That news couldn't have been shared in the worst possible way."

"Aunt Cr—"

"No, no." She lifted a hand. "Your dad stormed off in a snit, Lord knows why. It's not like he has a leg to stand on." Crystal turned to her nephew while Kait mulled over what the other woman could mean by that comment. "Or didn't you know you almost had an older brother?"

No, he hadn't known. Kait could see it in his eyes.

"It's why your dad and mom got married." She emphasized the words with a nod of her head. "But that's neither here nor there." She included both of them in her gaze. "The rest of the family is dying to hear the details. And I think I have a solution to at least one of your problems, or did you already rent a place in town?"

Shane shook his head.

"That's what I thought. There's the old ranch house by the south entrance. You'll live there."

"Aunt Crystal," Shane said, "that belongs to you and Uncle Bob."

"I know, I know. But it's not being used. We'd always planned to refurbish the place and give it to one of the boys, but they've all settled into their own places. It might be a little run-down but it'll do for you, at least until you figure something else out. And I'm sure we can come up with enough furniture to get you settled. We'll have it set up in a snap. I mean, you can't exactly let her live with you and your brothers and cousins in the bunkhouse."

Is that where he lived? With his family? Yet another thing she hadn't known.

"So now that's settled. Help your bride on up, Shane. We're holding an impromptu wedding reception out on the back porch and you two are the star attraction."

SHANE WOULD BE grateful to his aunt Crystal for the rest of his life. She ushered them out to the back porch with a wide smile on her face. "Here they are. The happy couple."

And it didn't matter that his dad was nowhere to be found. Nobody mentioned Kait's pregnancy. Everybody gave her a hug and wished them both well. Someone even went to the local store and came back with a cake.

Without his dad around, the tension on the patio had completely disappeared.

Afterward, everyone headed over to the home he'd be sharing with Kait. His aunt and sister swept and mopped the place. His brothers scoured the ranch for extra furniture. By the time the sun went down, they were settled into their new home, and Shane had to admit it was a huge relief to know he had a place for them both.

"Your family is nice," Kait said.

Everyone except his dad. He tried not to think about his dad and how he had disappeared. He was probably down at the barn working with one of his cutting horses. That was what he did when his temper flared. He'd done it all the time when his mom had been alive. Their arguments had always ended with a door slamming and his dad disappearing for hours. His mom had often said at least he didn't go to a bar to cool off. His mom had always been gracious and understanding.

"What?" she asked. "What did I say?"

Only then did he realize his face reflected the sadness of his thoughts. "Just thinking about my mom."

They had settled at the kitchen table someone had found somewhere and that had clearly seen better days with its scarred surface and spindly wooden legs. He wondered what Kait thought about the tiny house his aunt and uncle had provided for them. Probably not what she was used to given her high-dollar career and famous family back in North Carolina. Their lives had been completely flipped on their ends. But Kait hadn't complained. She'd taken everything in her stride, and if he were honest, he admired the hell out of her for it.

"Tell me about her."

Thinking about his mom hurt. Not a day went by that

he didn't picture her face or hear her voice in his head. She'd truly been the yin to his dad's yang. If she'd still been alive, his dad would never have gotten away with storming off. Never.

"She was an angel."

There was no better way to describe her. She'd put up with so much from his dad. As a kid, he'd lived in fear that she would walk out on them, but she'd stuck it out. Now that he knew the reason for her marriage to his dad, it all made a little more sense. Still, there was a part of him that wondered if the stress of being married to Reese Gillian hadn't contributed to her early death. Stress could lead to all kinds of health problems.

"When did she die?"

"Seven years ago."

He'd been in the midst of qualifying for his first NFR. Hip deep in a rodeo season that'd been brutal between bad weather and wounded horses. He'd almost had it done—been right on the cusp of the qualifying bubble—when his sister had called, bawling, admitting that their mom had gone in for emergency surgery… and never woken up.

He shot up from his chair. His brothers had stocked their refrigerator with a six-pack of beer. He went and grabbed one and almost offered one to Kait before remembering she was pregnant. He popped the lid and took a swig before turning to her.

"You want anything?"

She shook her head, and she looked beautiful sitting there with the light of a lamp illuminating one side of her face, the red top she wore setting the curve of her bare shoulders aglow. The shirt clung to her curves and showed off her figure. Nobody would even know she was pregnant. Her jeans still hugged her hips and flattened her tummy, and he couldn't help but think he was a very lucky man. She might be famous, but she didn't act it, not at all.

"Look," he said, taking a seat, "I'll sleep on the couch tonight. You can take the bed. In the morning, we'll sort out our travel arrangements to North Carolina."

She nodded and he had to admit to disappointment. He knew this wasn't a real marriage and yet there was a part of him that...

What?

Hoped they could make it work? Why? He'd always sworn off women. Yet here he was wondering if there was any way a woman like Kait could fall for an average-Joe cowboy like him.

"Thanks." She peered up at him with her big blue eyes. "I think I'll turn in now."

He didn't say anything, just nodded, then took another swig of his beer. For the first time in his life, he was tempted to drink his troubles away.

"Good night."

She stood, turned away, and his mouth opened, his vocal cords tightening as he fought the urge to call her name.

He didn't.

Instead, he watched her walk away.

Chapter Eight

Kait awoke from a sleep so deep that at first she didn't know where she was when she opened her eyes. Then it came back to her.

Las Vegas. Gillian Ranch. Shane.

Her phone trilled. She sat up in bed, but when she caught sight of the boldfaced text that spelled out who was calling, she sucked in a deep breath.

Dad.

She didn't want to answer but she'd never been a coward. Clutching the covers up around her, she reluctantly pressed the accept-call button.

"Hi, Daddy."

The use of the pet name was instinctive, something she'd done since she was a little girl when she knew she was in trouble and sought to sweet-talk him. It didn't work.

"Have you seen the front page of ProRacing.com?"

It felt like someone had slapped her with a defibrillator, because she knew where this was headed.

"You need to look," said her dad in as stern a voice as she'd ever heard, and it was amazing because she was a grown woman, and yet he could make her feel five years old all over again.

"I don't have internet," she admitted.

"Then let me read it to you."

No. Please. Don't. She didn't want to know.

"'Stockcar's Supergirl Knocked Up.'"

Oh, dear goodness. It was worse than she'd thought. She'd been thinking someone had leaked her getting married, not this.

"My phone's been ringing off the hook."

Who? Who would leak this? Someone in her doctor's office back in North Carolina? That had to be it.

"I'm so sorry, Dad."

"And then I hear from your mom that she knew about it all along."

She clutched the phone. "She only found out yesterday."

"That's one day ahead of me, and I had to find out from a sportszine."

And he was angry. She didn't blame him.

"Do you have any idea how many résumés I've received so far today?"

She was sure at least fifty. Word spread fast when there was an opening with a top team, and Cooper Racing was about as good as it could get.

"I'm sending the jet for you."

"Wait, what? No, Dad. You don't have to do that. I was planning on coming home this week, anyway."

"You told Amanda you'd be home yesterday."

She twisted so she sat on the edge of the bed, tried to calm her rattled nerves because she had sort of fudged the truth with her publicity agent. "That was the plan, but things sort of…got out of hand."

"You got married."

She winced. "I did."

And then her father's voice changed. He pitched it lower, his words barely audible. "I never would have thought you would want to walk down the aisle without me."

Kait closed her eyes, a hot flush of shame turning her cheeks red. "I'm so sorry, Daddy."

She heard him take a deep breath. "Chuck said he can be there by noon your time. He said there's an airport by the coast with a jet center. Be there by noon."

"You don't have to have Chuck fly all the way out here."

"It wasn't a suggestion. I want you home."

She winced again. "Okay."

"And bring your new husband."

He hung up before she could explain that it wasn't like that. Shane couldn't just take off. But it was clear her father didn't want to hear it.

"Was that your dad?"

She looked up and there he was. Shane, standing in her doorway without his shirt on, a hint of hair on his chest, the strands thicker by the waistband of his jeans.

Don't go there.

"Yes." She stood up, felt woozy for a moment, but it was just stress.

"You okay?"

He'd crossed the room without her noticing, his blue eyes full of concern. Without his cowboy hat and with stubble staining his chin and his dusky sideburns, he looked like something from a website specializing in hot men. She had to look away because she suddenly felt self-conscious in her T-shirt and underwear. Ridiculous, stupid thing to think given their current circumstances.

"Fine. Just disappointed in myself."

He reached for her hand, and, as always happened when he touched her, electricity danced up her arms. The chemistry between them couldn't be denied, but she needed to keep it under wraps because the last thing she needed was to develop feelings for him. They would be living apart one day soon. She frowned as she recalled her conversation with her father. Maybe sooner than they thought.

"Don't be disappointed in yourself," he said. "We've both made mistakes. We'll deal with it together."

She finally had herself under control, enough that she could look him in the eye without him seeing something she didn't want him to see. Humiliation. That was what she sought to keep from him.

"He's sending a jet."

Shane's brows lifted. "Your family owns a jet?"

"Of course. All the big teams have them."

He clearly hadn't known that, and she wondered what else he didn't know about stock-car racing. He'd never admitted to recognizing her the first night they'd met, although, to be honest, she hadn't asked, hadn't cared. But now she wondered if he had known who she was.

"He wants you to come home with me."

He straightened. "I told you, I have a job here to do. And a rodeo to practice for. And things to pack and unpack from the last trip on the road."

"It'd just be for a day or two. Maybe your brother could help out."

She could tell by the way he frowned that he didn't want to ask anyone for help. Pride. He had it in scores. That was the kind of man he was. She admired that about him.

"Please?"

He took a deep breath, his eyes softening, and she knew she'd won. It was such a relief that she took a deep breath, too. "Thank you."

"Just promise me your dad won't meet us at the airport with a shotgun."

She crossed her heart. "I promise."

SHANE HAD HEARD about private jets. Hell, some of his rough-stock rider pals liked to charter them from time to time in order to hit more rodeos, but as a "timey," too, he didn't have the luxury of hopping on a plane, not unless charter jets could carry his horse. So to say he felt as uncomfortable as a baby chick in a room full of cats was an understatement. It didn't help that they'd been greeted at the base of the twin engine's stairs by a man who'd greeted Kait by name. "Chuck" had smiled and offered his congratulations. Clearly, there was some history there.

"At least I didn't have to fly back home commercial," she said as she settled on a plush leather seat. He took the one opposite and the thing damn near swallowed him whole.

"I could definitely get used to this," he said with a smile.

She nodded, pulling out her phone and tapping at some keys. She'd done that the whole way to the airport, too, and he tried not to be offended. He knew she had a busy life. Heck, her star was certainly higher than his own, but he couldn't help but think something had changed since her conversation with her dad. She seemed more closed off. Less…warm.

When the jet pushed away from the tarmac, he expected her to look up, but she didn't. He cocked his black cowboy hat back so he could stare out the window better, watching as they approached the runway. They were on some sort of preferential take-off list because, in a matter of seconds, the engines had powered up and they were sailing down a strip of asphalt that gleamed like the surface of a river in the afternoon sunshine. It was one of the perfectly clear days on the coast. The ground raced by faster and faster, and then his belly seemed to dip toward his feet as they took off.

It was his favorite part of flying, Shane's nose pressed to the window and as they gained altitude, he spotted the ocean to his left. They banked, heading out over the Pacific. It shimmered beneath them like a bottle of glitter that had spilled on a dark blue carpet. He turned to tell Kait. She'd leaned her head back on her seat, and as he stared at her he noticed the sun painted the one side of her face like a Rembrandt. Her blond hair was loose around her shoulders and she looked timelessly beautiful in that moment. He watched as the lines on her forehead relaxed. Saw the way her shoulders slipped down. Spotted her hand sliding off the arm of the chair and into her lap.

Asleep.

Just like that. He glanced out the window again. *She is probably used to this*, he thought. Probably thought nothing of taking off on a small jet and of the view down below because she'd seen it a hundred times.

There were no flight attendants, but Kait had explained he could help himself to the refrigerator in the back. He'd met the pilot and copilot before they'd taken off, but the two men seemed content to stay in the cockpit. He turned back to the window, alone with his thoughts. So many emotions coursed through him as he thought about meeting her parents. Anticipation. Curiosity. Dread.

He awoke with a start what must have been hours later, surprised to realize he'd dozed off. It had to have been the sound of the engines, because they'd changed, and he realized they were dropping altitude. Not only that, but the sun had started to set. A quick glance at his cell phone revealed the time had automatically changed.

"Are we there?" She sat up, her eyes still soft with sleep.

"Looks like we'll be landing shortly."

She rubbed her eyes, looking no less adorable with her hair mussed from her long nap and a crease across her right cheek. She must have sensed his gaze because she tried to smooth down the wayward strands.

"I fell asleep."

He smiled. "I was thinking maybe we ought to approach your parents a bit differently than we did my family."

"What do you mean?"

He shrugged a bit. "You know, do what we talked about that first day. Tell your people we're in love. Ham it up a bit."

She didn't seem convinced, not surprising, given the way he'd broken the news to his own family. She was probably worried the two families would talk.

"It's not like my family's going to meet your family anytime soon, if that's what you're worried about. There's no way they'll find out we have a marriage of convenience."

She smiled a bit. "What an antiquated way of putting it."

He shrugged. "It applies though, doesn't it?"

She nodded and looked out the window, the yellow half glow of the setting sun turning her hair gold. She'd pulled it all to one side and it swirled around like a soft-serve ice-cream cone.

And you've lost your mind making metaphors like that.

"Maybe it'll work."

Why did his heart leap? Pretending to be in love wasn't going to be easy. Maybe that was it. Maybe his heart had sped up out of dread.

"Think about it. We don't have to make any decisions until we get to your parents' house."

"Actually, that's not true."

He tensed. He knew what she was about to say even before she said it.

"They're meeting us at the airport."

Of course they were.

"But I can give you my answer now. Honestly, I'll do anything to soften the blow of my dad's disappointment, and if we can convince him we're in love, he'll be a lot more understanding. He fell head over heels for my mom so he'll have no room to talk."

It happened again. His heart flipped inside his chest. And it wasn't dread, he realized. It was anticipation. He looked forward to getting closer to her, even if it was all pretend.

And that scared the hell out of him.

Chapter Nine

The wedding ring felt strange on her finger. She kept fiddling with it. Nerves, she supposed, because she was terrified about seeing her parents.

Shane's right. It'll be better if they think we're in love.

She just wasn't convinced she could pull it off, especially when she kept sneaking glances at Shane. He looked like some kind of rock-star cowboy in his black hat, black shirt and black jeans, the scruff of stubble having grown darker since yesterday. She wondered if he'd forgotten to shave, but she had to admit the look suited him, and that made her all the more uncomfortable because she shouldn't be noticing things like that. She should be keeping her distance. Instead she'd have to touch him and be close to him and look lovingly into his eyes, all the while keeping her emotions in check because she couldn't let their attraction get out of hand. It seemed an impossible task, but she had no choice. Their physical connection to each other didn't matter. She had his name and a ring on her finger, and that would be enough…at least for her parents.

She turned her gaze out the window. Between cotton-candy clouds, she caught a glimpse of the familiar topog-

raphy of the state she loved gliding beneath her. Patches
of thick trees were intersected by small cities and towns.
North Carolina's subtropical climate provided a steady
stream of moisture for Lake Wylie, which glistened like
a neon snake in a green lawn.

Home.

"You ready for this?"

"As ready as I'll ever be."

All too quickly, the jet touched down. It was both a
blessing and a curse that they taxied so quickly to the jet
center. She knew Lance and Sarah Cooper would greet
her at the airport and there they were, standing behind
a wall of glass in the jet center's reception area. Her
stomach dropped to her toes. Her dad looked as stern
as a law-enforcement officer, his arms crossed, his lips
in a straight line as, a few minutes later, he watched her
descend the jet's narrow stairs.

"You okay?" asked her new husband, staring up at
her and holding out a hand to steady her.

"Fine."

He must have seen her parents, too, because he pulled
her up alongside him the moment she had both feet on
the tarmac. He even smiled down at her and when he
did, her brain just sort of went, "Ooo," and she gulped
and looked away.

Why did she have to be so attracted to him?

He pulled her even closer so their hips were touching and then her view disappeared because he touched
his lips to hers and it all came back…every crazy reaction she'd ever had to his touch. Goosebumps. Stomach
butterflies. Body tingles. All of it.

"It'll be okay," he whispered in her ear.

Such goodness in his eyes. It was one of the things

that most attracted her to him. And, yes, damn it, he still did it for her, and that was so disconcerting that she had to close her eyes. Shane kept her heading in the right direction, even though it took every ounce of her willpower to keep her feet moving.

"Smile," he gently ordered.

She opened her eyes and did exactly that, even though her feet matched rhythm with her heart. Bump. Bump. Bump. Bump.

"My baby," said her mom the moment she entered the air-conditioned waiting area. Warm arms enveloped her, and for the first time in a long, long time, Kait felt in need of her mother's comfort. But eventually her mother leaned back, peering into her eyes intently, searching her gaze as if silently asking her how she could keep such a big secret from her best friend. It was all Kait could do to hold her mom's gaze.

"I'm going to be a grandmother," Sarah Cooper said, the copper curls that she'd been so famous for in her youth slightly tinged by premature gray, but only a little. "My baby is having a baby."

"Hi," said Shane. "I'm Shane Gillian."

Kait turned in time to see Shane hold out his hand to her dad, who just stared at it. Warmth spread through her cheeks because she'd known it would be this way. Her dad was nothing if not a conservative, and a shotgun marriage combined with a surprise pregnancy was probably right up there with working at a strip club—at least in his eyes.

"We need to talk." Her dad's gaze captured her own and she hated the look on his face. Here was the man who'd once bandaged her knees and kissed her on the nose and told her that she could be anything when she grew up, including a race-car driver. Now? He seemed so disillusioned. It stabbed her right in the gut.

"Daddy, can't it wait?"

Her dad's stern blue eyes brooked no argument. "And I'd like to talk to you without your…" She saw him swallow. Hard. "Husband."

Okay, so now she felt about three years old.

"Lance, really," said her mother, her kind blue eyes filled with concern. "Can we do this at home?"

He looked at her mom with the eyes of a dragon. "No."

Kait glanced at Shane, shooting him a look of apology, but the man just smiled in silent reassurance and it was such a look of understanding she felt her insides turn to goo He cared for her. Really, really cared for her.

"Outside," her dad snapped.

"Actually, sir," said Shane with an apologetic smile, "I feel I should be in on this conversation.

If her dad had dragon eyes before, they changed into crocodile eyes right then. "Really?"

"Yes, sir."

Her estimation of the man she'd married went up another notch. It was clear Shane wasn't afraid of her dad. He pulled his shoulders back. Stood toe to toe. He even lifted his chin up, the brim of the cowboy hat no longer shielding his eyes.

"Fine," said her father. "We'll do this at home."

Lance Cooper had always been a pretty easygoing man. His famous sense of humor was legendary in the world of racing. You wouldn't know it now.

Shane took her hand. She held on to it for dear life. Her mom and dad led the way out of the jet center. They'd brought the SUV, a gift from a local dealership.

The interior smelled of leather and pine spray when Shane pulled open the door.

"It'll be okay," he quietly whispered as he helped her into the vehicle.

When she looked into his eyes all she saw was concern. "Thank you."

She barely noticed the familiar streets they passed. She felt more than saw Shane shift in his seat next to her. When she glanced over at him, his arms were held toward her, his invitation obvious. He flipped up the drink holder between them, scooted toward the edge of his seat. She did the same, resting her head on his shoulder. She caught a glimpse of her father's eyes in the rearview mirror. It prompted her to close her own eyes, the sun flickering across her face as they passed by trees and buildings.

That was the last thing she remembered.

"SHE'S ASLEEP."

Shane looked into the eyes of the pretty woman who stared at him from the front seat of the SUV. Kait's mom smiled.

"She's been sleeping a lot." And he had to admit it worried him.

"Poor thing looks exhausted." But her mom didn't seem concerned, just turned back to stare out the front as they made their way to the Cooper household. "I slept a lot, too, at the beginning of my pregnancies."

He shifted a bit and, in the rearview mirror, caught a glimpse of Kait's dad. The man didn't seem pleased. For a moment, Shane lost himself in the sheer craziness of staring into Lance Cooper's eyes. He'd been awestruck when he'd first met Kait, but that was nothing compared to meeting the famous race-car driver. He'd grown up watching him on TV. Had seen his infomercial for that space-age motor oil at least a million times. To be honest, one of the reasons he'd so easily recognized Kait was because of his hero worship of her dad, and now Lance Cooper *hated* him.

"Here we are," Kait's mother said as they passed through a wrought-iron gate with a metal cutout of a race car on it. Trees lined the driveway and between them, off in the distance, he spotted the twinkling sparkles of a lake. But then his attention caught on the massive stone structure that seemed to pop up in front of them. His jaw dropped.

Kait's mother must have glanced back. "Don't let it fool you. Inside, it's just a home."

Somehow he doubted it. He'd seen some pretty spectacular homes over the years. Some of their clients were pretty rich. Heck, his own family was wealthy, but this place was like something out of a travel book, one titled *Stone Homes of Europe* or something. Stained-glass windows were intermixed with regular ones. They were set into light gray stones that covered a massive front wall. In the middle, set beneath an A-frame entryway, were double doors, wood, each inlaid with sparkling crystal glass.

Lance shut off the engine. They all sat in the vehicle a second as Shane debated what to do.

The decision was taken out of his hands.

"Are we here?"

The sleepy murmur of Kait's voice caught everyone's attention. Her eyes opened at the same time as she sat up, peering out the front windshield, her face softening when she caught sight of her childhood home.

"Lance, I think they should both rest for a bit before we have our big powwow."

Lance cocked his head in his wife's direction, eyebrow lifted, and Shane could tell he didn't like the idea.

"No." Kait wiped at her eyes. "I'm awake now."

He had a feeling she just wanted to get it over with. He didn't blame her, but as they exited the car, he wondered how he could ever hope to compete with…all this. His eyes darted over the perfectly manicured lawn in front of the house, catching the gorgeous lake behind, then back to the home that stood two-stories tall in some places.

"I want to head back to my place before it gets too dark."

He'd told her he'd act the caring husband but, to be honest, it wasn't much of an act as he helped her out of the SUV. She really did seem exhausted, even though she'd slept for hours already, and once again he felt a little shiver of concern.

"You okay?" he asked, placing an arm around her shoulder.

She looked up at him, and he could tell the moment she remembered they were supposed to be playing a part because she visibly changed in front of his eyes. Her shoulders relaxed. Her eyes softened. He found himself leaning toward her without any thought and before he could tell himself to slow down, kissed her.

"Now, now," said her mom. "Enough of that. Let's get inside so we can figure all this out."

Kait drew back, but she still stared up at him in the strangest way as she said, "Figure what out?"

"How you're going to make a living. What role you'll

play at Cooper Racing now. And then later, how you're going to drive cars and raise a kid."

Kait's face crumpled.

"I think I should probably be in on this conversation, too," Shane said. "Kait's my wife and she's carrying my baby." He pinned Lance with a stare. "And your grandchild. How we move forward should be a group decision."

He watched as Kait's dad visibly tried to calm himself down. The man was clearly upset and angry and disappointed in his daughter, and if Shane could read that on his face, he was sure Kait could, too. One look into her eyes and he could see that she did see it.

"Dad, please," she said softly. "Let's all go inside and talk."

Lance Cooper stared at the group of people around him, but his gaze settled on his daughter, and in his eyes Shane saw the displeasure fade into something like embarrassment and then acceptance. Movement caught Lance's attention and Shane realized Kait's mother was staring at her husband, arms crossed, foot tapping, the expression on her face akin to a yard monitor admonishing a pupil on the playground.

"Fine. Let's go inside."

Chapter Ten

"You going to stay out here all night?"

Kait half turned and saw Shane's form outlined by the lights on inside her house, his face in darkness. She didn't need to look into his eyes to know what was on his face. Concern. She could hear it in his voice.

"When I was a kid, my parents would let us camp out as a special treat. I remember being lulled to sleep by the sound of the waves." She turned back, watching as the waves caught beams of moonlight, silvering the tips. "I miss those days."

She heard rather than saw him move up alongside her, taking a seat on the bench she'd placed at the lake's edge just for this purpose.

"It'll all work out. You'll see."

And it would. Once her dad had settled down, they'd worked through a lot of issues with the racing business. Her dad already had a replacement driver in mind. He'd wanted to know when she'd return to work. She'd explained that her first doctor's appointment would be this week and she'd know more then. That started a whole other conversation about where she'd live and who'd be delivering the baby and a whole host of other question she'd shoved to the back of her mind. It had been a crazy weekend. Looked like it would be a crazy week, too.

"We don't have to keep doing this if you don't want."

She could see him better now. Her eyes had adjusted to the darkness, but it didn't help her mood any to have company. She'd let her family down and it was eating her up inside.

"I wish." She shook her head. "The only reason my dad didn't kill me today is because he thinks you and I are in love, and my fans will, too, once our PR department sends out a press release. We have to keep this up."

He didn't say anything, and when she glanced at him she noted he looked deep in thought.

"I'm sorry about today," she said. "It couldn't have been easy sitting through all that."

"No, actually. I learned a lot about racing."

"Yeah. Fifty things you didn't need to know about the stock-car circuit."

"No. It was interesting. I had no idea race-car drivers did so much. I mean, I knew you appeared in public and stuff, but I didn't know you were in on design meetings and that you did PR appearances away from the track. I just sort of thought you…" Even in the dark she could see him shrug. "…drove."

She smiled. It had an odd effect, that smile. She started to relax, started the think that maybe, just maybe, her world wasn't ending.

"It actually didn't go as bad as I thought."

"Your parents clearly love you."

They did, which was probably why it stung so much to let them down. "I going to miss them while we're in California."

They'd told her parents she planned to travel between

the two coasts for now. Shane would continue his life on the rodeo circuit. She would perform whatever duties she could for as long as she could. It would be a crazy life, but they could handle it…together.

And that was part of why she'd come outside—to analyze how conflicted she felt and not just because she hated disappointing her parents but because Shane had sat next to her during the entire meeting, supporting her, holding her hand. He'd given her strength she didn't even know she needed, and it worried her.

It was an act, remember?

"Are you sure you want to head back to California tomorrow?" he asked.

"You heard my dad. They have things under control. If we're going to put down stakes, it's probably better to do it now. You have a career to think of and I…" She had to swallow in order to get the word out. "…don't."

She felt his hand fall on her own and she almost pulled her hand away. "You're having a baby, not getting both legs removed. And you heard your dad. Your job will be there once the baby is born."

And there he went again. The voice of reason.

"Relax," he said, jiggling her hand. "Let's take it one day at a time."

He was a good man. The more time she spent with him, the more she admitted things could have been so much worse.

"Your dad is pretty amazing, by the way." He released her hand and it troubled her even more to note how deflated she felt once he let her go. "I can't get over how surreal it was to meet someone I've looked up to my entire life."

She cocked her head at him. "You follow my dad?"

"On Facebook, Twitter and Instagram." Even in the dark, she could see his teeth flash as he smiled. "I'm surprised you didn't see the Star Oil die-cast car that was on my shelf in my old room."

She'd had no idea. But then, it wasn't exactly something that would normally come up in conversation. Oddly enough, the realization that he followed her dad's racing career made her heart soften all the more.

"You're lucky to have them."

She was, and she knew it, especially after watching Shane's relationship with his dad. Thank goodness he had the rest of his family.

And her.

It hit her then. Really hit her. She'd be a part of his life forever.

"I think I'm going to turn in."

He started to stand. She reached for his hand before he could do more than get his legs beneath him.

"Thank you."

He turned to look at her and the mood changed. Just like that. A snap of the fingers. A beat of the heart. Electricity danced between them.

She knew it then, knew it with an absolute certainty. She could have a real future with this man. If only that were possible.

"You're welcome," he said softly.

And then he was gone, her hand dropping to her side on the bench, her heart beating as loudly as his footfalls on the brick path he'd followed to her side.

WHAT A CLOSE CALL.

Shane all but ran back inside. It took all his willpower not to barricade his door once he made it back to his guest room.

Guest room.

She had a home that belonged on a television show. Not as lavish as her parents', but still better than anything he would be able to afford. It was the sad truth that rodeo cowboys didn't make millions of dollars. Life on the road was expensive. Over the years, he'd been able to put away some of the bigger purses. He had just about enough to purchase some land from his dad, but he'd never be able to afford a home like Kait's.

Millions. That was what she made. He'd married America's sweetheart of the stock-car circuit and damned if he didn't feel completely inadequate sitting in her luxurious home after sharing a meal with her famous parents. Tomorrow they would hop on a private jet—again—and head back to California where they would share a tiny little farmhouse on his aunt and uncle's land.

He heard her come in, not her footsteps, because the house was so big she'd have to be wearing clogs for him to hear footfalls. No. He heard the sliding back door open and close, knew she'd be walking by. It amazed him how hard it was to keep from going to the door. He wanted to step in front of her. To hold her again.

To kiss her.

Yes. That, too. There was no denying it. Where Kait was concerned, the sexual attraction was off the charts. There were times when he wished this were a real marriage and he could head off to bed with her so he could show her just exactly what she did to him. Instead, he forced himself to undress, to climb beneath the covers and try to get some sleep. But it was a longtime coming. All he could think about was Kait somewhere down the hall, alone.

He woke up tired and out of sorts the next morning, probably because he knew he was in for a boatload of work once he returned to the ranch. His brothers were always good at covering for him in a pinch, but they took it out of his hide once he was back in action. Coupled with the fact that he had a rodeo that weekend and he hadn't ridden in four days, well, he had a feeling he was in for a rough week.

"Ready?" Kait asked with a smile so false it should belong on the face of a used-car salesman.

"Ready," he said, hitching his duffel bag over his arm. It smelled faintly of horses. Not surprising, since it traveled to rodeos with him.

He took one last look around her elegant home and wondered if he'd ever see it again. This was a business arrangement, he reminded himself, kept reminding himself, because damn it all, when she looked as good as she did this morning it was hard to keep his eye on the ball. She wore an off-white blouse that clung to her trim frame and was so sheer it revealed the lacy shirt she had on beneath. She'd tucked it into a pair of jeans with rhinestones on the pockets and they hugged her curves in a way that made his eyes dip downward. You'd never know she was pregnant. Not even a little bit.

"The pilot called this morning to confirm our travel arrangements. We'll be back in California by noon, thanks to the time change."

"Good to know," he said, following her out. Amazing to have your own jet. He still marveled over it all. Even when they pulled up the airport, he still tried to take it all in. She'd been quiet the whole ride there and that didn't change once they boarded the twin-engine jet.

"I'm going to take a nap."

He wasn't surprised. It seemed that was all she ever wanted to do lately. And for a moment, he allowed himself some concern again. This week she'd see a doctor for the first time, and to be honest, he was glad.

He busied himself on the way home with planning his rodeos for the rest of the year, in between keeping an eye on Kait. She seemed restless. At one point she woke up, looked out the window, then went back to sleep again. They landed and they coasted to a stop in front of the Santa Barbara jet center.

"Look," she said when the stepped off the plane, "I did a lot of thinking last night."

Uh-oh. That sounded ominous.

"I was thinking maybe I should stay at your aunt and uncle's place. You can keep living with your brothers." He saw her take a deep breath. "You know, like you normally do."

He stopped at the base of the jet's staircase. In the distance, a big jet took off at the main airport and the sound deafened him so that he had to yell to be heard.

"No." It shocked him how quickly the word rose to his lips and how loudly he shouted it, far more loudly than he needed to, even over the sound of the Airbus's engine.

"No?" she repeated back.

A lock of her hair caught the wind, driven by the ocean just a few short miles away, and the scent of salt was hanging in the air.

"I just think it's best if we keep this more of a businesslike relationship."

No.

No, no, no.

But another part of him, the sane part of him, admitted it was a great idea. He already had feelings for her that he probably shouldn't. Last night had been evidence of that.

"No," he said again.

It was one of those moments when you know you should bite your tongue, but he just couldn't seem to do so. It was like being shot off the back of a bull. His stomach dropped. He stood for a moment, stunned. He really did have feelings for her.

"We should stick together, especially when we return to ranch. We're going to need each other in the coming weeks."

"What does it matter if we live apart? Nobody will know outside the ranch. It seems pretty secluded there. I doubt the paparazzi will be hiding in the trees. I'm just a race-car driver. Not a big deal in the scheme of things."

It *was* a big deal. *She* was a big deal—to him. And their living arrangements, too. Their unborn child. It all mattered. And he didn't want… He tried to gather his thoughts, because the truth was he didn't know what he wanted, but it sure wasn't what she suggested.

"We stick together," he said, heading for his truck. She didn't follow, and he turned back to argue his point even more but froze when he spotted the look on her face. She'd placed a hand on her belly, panic in her eyes, and when their gazes connected, hers was filled with panic.

"I think something's wrong."

Chapter Eleven

He'd never driven so fast in his life. Kait didn't seem to notice. She sat in the passenger seat of his truck, eyes closed, hand on her belly. She'd kept it there the entire time. As if she could hold their child inside her if something really were wrong.

"Almost there."

Fortunately, they were near a hospital. Unfortunately, she whimpered as he pulled into a spot. He'd never known skin could tingle while blood drained from someone's face, but that was exactly how it felt. Kait wasn't the type to cry out in pain. Tough as nails, that was his girl.

His girl?

Yes, damn it. They were a couple now no matter what. And she was scared right now. The pupils of her blue eyes were dilated and there were brackets around her mouth that he'd never seen before.

"Let's get you inside." He held out his hand. Her palms were sweaty.

He didn't want to lose the baby. It struck him like the horns of a bull, made his knees grow weak for a moment so that he stumbled a bit, forcing him to catch his breath. He feared for the tiny life inside of her, and for Kait, too.

They took her right in, stashing her in a curtained room, one with drapes that'd been left open and gave them a view of doctors rushing back and forth. Someone came in, a nurse of some sort, and the kind-eyed older woman had Kait change into a paper robe. Shane tried to help her but Kait waved him away, and even though he knew it was ridiculous, he kept his eyes averted. She finished quickly and Shane helped her settle back into the bed, although though she wanted to take a seat. Stubborn woman. He insisted on covering her with a blanket and then helping her adjust a pillow that reminded him of something you'd find on an airplane, except it was covered in paper.

"Thank you," she said, but the words were immediately followed by a grimace of pain.

"Do you need anything?"

She shook her head, and he admitted to himself he'd never felt so helpless in his life. His shoulders sagged in relief when a different nurse came in. This one was younger and far more no-nonsense, with her pulled-back hair and plain black smock. She checked Kait's vitals, and he found his hand sliding into Kait's as the dark-haired woman wrapped a blood-pressure cuff around her forearm. Kait clutched at his hand, and the coldness of it alarmed him. He didn't think she was the type to hold on to someone for help, but that was exactly what she did.

"Am I alive?" she joked with the nurse, who gave her a tight smile in response.

"You're fine."

So much for bedside manners. They both watched as

she entered information into her table. She gave them an impersonal smile before saying, "The doctor will be here shortly.

Shane smirked. He'd been in his fair share of emergency rooms over the years. No doctor ever arrived "shortly."

"I'm sorry," Kait whispered.

"Sorry?" He couldn't keep the disbelief from his voice. "Don't be silly, Kait. This isn't your fault."

"If I'd stayed at the ranch—"

"Don't. We don't even know what's wrong. It could be…" He racked his brain. "…indigestion. Or gas. It could be gas. You did eat that burrito for lunch yesterday. One good fart and you might be all better."

She stared at him in the same way the nurse had a moment before, but then he saw her face begin to fracture. Her lips lifted a bit.

"Very fun—"

"Hi, Kait," said a man, who shocked them both with his sudden appearance. He was staring at the tablet in his hand, but then he looked up and stopped dead in his tracks. "Kait Cooper." He glanced down at the electronic chart again. "You're Kaitlin Cooper."

Shane would have laughed at the doctor's slack jaw if they were in any other situation. The doctor recovered quickly, however, and glanced down at the chart again.

"You're having some cramping?"

She nodded.

The man came forward. "I'm Dr. Penrod, the ob-gyn on call."

"Kait," she said softly, forcing a smile, holding out her hand.

He shook Kait's hand, and something about the man's

bedside manner instantly reassured Shane. He was older with a ring of gray hair and shiny scalp that seemed to reflect the fluorescent lights above them.

"And how long as this been going on?"

"It just started."

The doctor nodded. "Okay then. Let's take a look." He moved Kait's robe off to the side, the paper crinkling at the movement. When he rested his hands on Kait's abdomen, his brows lifted.

"You said you're how many weeks pregnant?"

"Nine," she answered.

"Hmm." He kept probing, his face scrunched in concentration as he palpated Kait's belly. "Have you had an ultrasound yet?"

Kait shook her head.

Shane said, "She's supposed to be seen this week."

The doctor nodded, drew back. "Let's take a look now."

Shane met Kait's stare. Rather than reassured, she appeared more panicked than before. He squeezed her hand even harder.

The doctor came back in with a nurse, who pushed a machine in front of her. Kait's belly was exposed again. In a matter of minutes, the machine was on and the screen lit up with an image that looked more like a child's finger-painting experiment than the inside of a woman's body. He glanced at the doctor to gauge his reaction, his skin tingling again at the look on the man's face. He turned back to Kait.

"Are you sure you're only nine weeks?"

"Absolutely positive," she said.

The doctor moved the wand, and then his brows lifted. Shane was staring right at him when it happened.

He shifted the wand some more as, on screen, two little blobs came into focus.

"Well that explains that," the doctor said with a wide smile. "You're having twins."

TWENTY MINUTES LATER, Kait still reeled from the news.

"So I suspect you've just been overdoing it from the sound of things," the doctor was saying, his blue eyes peering sternly down at her. "The babies are fine. They each have a strong heartbeat. The cramps are just your body adjusting to what's going on in there. I'm going to urge you to stay off your feet for now. No flying back and forth. No hard exercise. No riding horses," he said with a wink at Shane.

Babies. That was the only word that stuck in Kait's head. Twins.

She felt light-headed.

"So she'll be okay if she rests?"

The doctor nodded. "Take her home and put her to bed, Dad."

"She already sleeps a lot."

"Perfectly normal. It's the hormones. Some women can barely stay awake. From everything I've seen today, she should be fine. A few days of off her feet and she'll be back at it. But let me know if the cramping gets worse or if any other symptoms develop."

The doctor went on to list the things she should be watching out for. Kait only half listened. Shane was nodding his head, clearly taking his roles as father-to-be and spouse seriously.

Twins.

"But they don't run in my family."

The men stopped talking. The doctor's smile grew. "It happens sometimes."

Twins.

She would never really remember getting dressed. The doctor ordered her discharge papers. Eventually, it was just the two of them alone in the partitioned-off area. She could watch feet pass by beneath the curtain and that entertained her for a moment while her mind tried to assimilate what they'd just been told.

"We're going to be okay," he said softly, reaching for her hand again. "I know this is a shock, but at least the babies are okay."

There was that word again. *Babies.* Two kids. Somehow that seemed so much worse than one. Then she felt instantly terrible for thinking children could be bad. She had been so panicked when she'd felt the initial twinge of pain. In that moment, she'd realized how dearly she held on to the tiny life inside her body.

"Not going to lie," Shane said. "You look like you want to cry."

No. She wasn't going to cry. Just because there were two lives inside of her instead of one didn't change how she felt. She would deal with having two children in the same way she dealt with everything. Head on.

"I'm fine," she said, wincing when she straightened again. The doctor said the cramping would go away once her body adjusted to the two tiny bodies inside her. "Ready?"

He drove them to his home and she was glad. It gave her time to compile a to-do list in her head. She checked off one item immediately—texting her mom.

Surprise! I'm having twins.

Her mother's response was immediate.

Hahaha. Very funny. But I'm glad to know you made it back safe and sound. I've been waiting to hear from you.

She always let her mom know when she was wheels on the ground, but today her first thought had been the baby inside of her. *Babies.* She would have to get used to saying that.

I'm not kidding, Mom.

She stared out at the passing scenery, always intrigued by the tall mountains that lined the coast. They were studded with granite stones and yucca plants.

Her phone chimed.

Call me.

On the heels of the text, though, came the sound of her phone ringing, and she knew who it was. When she glanced at Shane, he smiled slightly, and she knew he'd figured out who she'd been texting.

"You're kidding, right?" Her mom's voice sounded as breathless as a marathon runner's. "Last I heard, you didn't even know your due date. You can't possibly know you're having twins."

"Actually, I do know." She filled her mother in on where she'd been for the past few hours. "We're on our way back to the ranch."

Her mother didn't say anything. Kait knew she was trying to assimilate the information.

"I'm flying out."

"What?" She leaned forward a bit. "Mom, you don't have to do that. I'm fine for now."

"You're doing too much. You need to rest. I'm telling your dad you're not to fly back home until you get a clean bill of health."

"Mom. I'll be fine."

"I don't care what you think. I know how you are. You'll keep going and going until you drop, but you can't do that now. You're carrying a baby. Babies," her mother quickly corrected. "Did the doctor say you could resume normal activity?"

"Wellll…"

"I'm flying out in the morning. I have a few things I'll have to wrap up here, but I'll be out there no later than noon."

"Mom—"

"I'll let you know when I get there. Text me the address."

"Mom!"

"I don't want to hear it, Kaitlin. This isn't your choice. This is my choice. As the grandmother of your future babies, I want to help. See you tomorrow."

She hung up before Kait could say another word.

"What's going on?" Shane asked.

Kait stared at the phone. "She's flying out here."

His brows lifted.

"Shane, she'll want to stay with us."

"So?"

"So? That means she'll be watching our every move."

And at last he caught on. "Meaning we'll have to go back to acting like we're in love."

"And sharing a room and dealing with your family and my mom interacting with your family, which means they'll tell her they'd never heard of me before last weekend. And then there'll be fifty thousand questions from my mom about why no one had heard of me and why we got married so quickly and..."

"Relax."

She was about to go on, but he touched her knee, and as he stared at her, his eyes went soft. She clung to his gaze as though she rode a buoy in a sea of uncertainty. *How does he do that?* she wondered. How could he soothe her with just a soft touch and a simple smile?

"It'll be okay."

She wished she were as confident.

Chapter Twelve

She'd never felt so useless in her life.

"You are not to overdo it," her mother said, her red curls bouncing as she bobbed her head to emphasize her words. "I don't care what you think, you shouldn't be going to a rodeo."

Kait released a sigh and grabbed her purse. Her mom had settled in for the long haul. Contrary to the doctor's prediction, her cramping hadn't gone away. A visit to a local ob-gyn had raised concerns that she might lose the babies if she didn't keep her activity down to a minimum. That was all her mom needed to hear. She'd called North Carolina, canceled her plans for the next few weeks and gotten a hotel room in town. The good news was she was only around during the day, and it was usually while Shane was at work, which meant their acting skills hadn't really been tested. The bad news was she insisted on following Kait around everywhere, like she was doing today. They were off to watch Shane compete at a rodeo, something her mom had very nearly forbidden her to do, but Kait couldn't wait to get out of the house. She missed the buzz of the racetrack and being in the action, and she was sincerely looking forward to watching Shane compete.

"I told you, Mom, sitting in a car and then some grandstands is no different than lounging around here."

Her mom grabbed her own purse off the counter. "That's what you think, but you heard the doctor on Thursday. You need to stay off your feet as much as possible."

Kait was pretty certain that her mom would chain her to a bed if she could. She took her job as nursemaid seriously. There were times when Kait could cheerfully kill her, but she honestly didn't know what she would have done without her this week. Her mother had arranged for a cleaning service to give their tiny new home a makeover. Next, she'd insisted on helping to furnish the place. Kait had wanted to pay, but that hadn't gone over well with Shane, who, as it turned out, had very traditional views on who should be the breadwinner in a family. He'd scored major bonus points with her mom. They'd given back everything but a gorgeous wood coffee table that Shane's brother, Carson, had made. It was too beautiful to give up.

"I'll be off my feet."

Feeling like a fat cow in jeans that are too tight.

"I'll be sitting in the passenger seat and then sitting in the grandstands." In a blousy shirt that she used to think emphasized her trim figure but now looked more like a circus tent.

"Just the same, I want you to be extra careful, and if you feel even the slightest twinge, you're to let me know."

They emerged into the bright California sunshine. It was something she could really get used to, this constant barrage of sunshine and the cooler climate. They were so close to the ocean that even if it did warm up during the day, it always cooled down at night thanks to coastal fog and an ocean breeze that somehow managed to climb the tall mountains to the west. They were headed to an event about three hours away in a small town called Clovis and to a rodeo Shane said was one of the biggest and best in the nation. Shane had left the night before, saying something about his brother needing a team-roping partner. She'd learned then that Shane did some team roping to help supplement his income. She hadn't even known Shane knew how to do that, much less that he was good enough to compete, but she'd said her goodbyes last night as he headed off to a Friday evening performance—or perf, as he called it—at a nearby competition. He'd insisted she stay at home, and so she'd heard via a text message that he and his brother had ended up second last night. Today they'd be roping again, trying for their share of a $20,000 purse but more important, riding bulls later that night.

Her tummy fluttered at the thought of him getting atop a two-thousand-pound bull. It was a unique experience. Usually she was the one doing something dangerous. Tonight she'd get a taste of what her mom went through every time she climbed behind the wheel of a car.

"I brought you a blanket and a pillow," said her mom, settling into the driver's seat of her rental car. "There's water in the backseat and I brought an extra phone charger. It's right there in case you want to plug your phone in."

Kait stared at the spotless dash and the charging nub where a cord hung and shook her head. How had her mom done it all those years—been the support group for the whole family, watching not one person you loved but three of them, up until her father had retired, get behind the wheel of a race car?

"You didn't have to do that."

"Push your seat back and sleep."

And now here she was, supporting her in another way. Damn, she was grateful to have her.

She didn't want to sleep, though. She'd done enough of that in the past week to last her a lifetime. Her mom said to store it all up, that she'd need all her reserves in a few months. She really didn't want to think about that.

"Did Shane arrive all right?"

Her mom glanced at her quickly before backing away from the quaint little ranch home Kait had been sharing with Shane this week, and the less she thought about Shane the better. Being in close quarters with him served as a constant reminder of their attraction to each other. He'd kept his distance, but there had been times when she'd wished....

"You look worried."

She glanced at her mom, her mouth opening to tell her mom she was just worried about Shane riding. Her mom would understand that, especially since they were supposedly in love, but as she was about to say the words, she fell silent instead. She was tired of it all, she realized. Tired of being worried about her babies. Tired of the charade. Tired of trying to understand why she felt so let down every time Shane settled on the couch at night. Why she tossed and turned not because she was in pain but because the father of those babies had been keeping his distance all week.

"Kait?" her mom prompted.

She took a deep breath. "I've been lying to you, Mom."

Sarah glanced at her in puzzlement. "What do you mean, honey?"

It took a few more gulps of oxygen before she could say, "It's all a sham, Mom. Our so-called happy marriage. How we fell in love. Our joy at my being pregnant. It's not real. Well, except for the part about the baby. Babies, I mean. I genuinely want to have him… her…them."

To her complete shock, her mom smiled and said, "Oh, sweetie, I knew all that."

Kait's mouth dropped open.

She nodded, eyes focused on the road ahead. "I'm not a complete fool, you know. You tell me everything. The fact that you kept your so-called relationship with this man to yourself told me something was up. And then I saw the two of you together and I'll admit you put on a good show, but you can't fool me."

She closed her mouth, but only for a second. "Does Dad know?"

"Goodness, no." Her mom shook her head, her face in profile as she drove. "He's on a need-to-know basis right now. I didn't want to add to his stress on top of everything else."

That *everything* being her bailing from the first race of the year and the fact that she could no longer drive for the rest of the season. That was the other thing. She hadn't known how much she'd miss strapping herself into a race car until it was gone.

Not forever, she quietly thought, patting her belly.

Her mom caught the motion. "I'm proud of you for keeping them, Kait. A lot of women wouldn't, you know."

"I could never get rid of them."

Her mom reached out and touched her hand. "I know that." She shot her a smile. "So we'll keep you here in California. Or maybe not. You could just chuck it all and admit the truth. There are bigger scandals in the news media, I'm sure."

"No," Kait said. "I'll be doing enough damage to my career by sitting out a year. The only thing I have right now is my untarnished image. I won't risk that."

"We don't live in the dark ages anymore, honey. This isn't the '50s. Women get pregnant out of wedlock all the time."

"We've already set the stage, Mom. To back out of it all now would make things seem even more tawdry. No. I'm going to stick it out."

But for how long? The question had been plaguing her. So had her crazy reaction to Shane sleeping on the couch all week. Why did she feel so…let down? The doctor had said everything could still go on as usual. She just needed to take it easy as much as possible.

"I'm here for you, you know."

And it was all she could do to swallow back a sudden lump in her throat. "I know."

Her mom lapsed into silence but Kait didn't mind. It gave her time to think. This week had given her a new perspective. One, she absolutely, unequivocally wanted to be a mom. No doubt. Two, she had feelings for Shane, and not just the you're-the-father-of-my-unborn-babies type of feelings. Oh, no. It went much deeper than that. Each night when she went to bed, she'd been filled with a longing she couldn't explain. She hated that she couldn't control those feelings. Couldn't just will them away somehow.

It scared her to death.

"Things have a way of working out."

Not this. She'd gotten pregnant by a near stranger, and now that man didn't want a thing to do with her, apparently. And then the babies would be here before they knew it and she'd be gone. Best to keep her feelings to herself.

Her mom patted her hand. "Chin up. You'll get through this."

Yes, but would she survive with her sanity intact? That was the question.

THE PLACE WAS PACKED, Shane admitted to himself. Not unusual given they were at one of the richest rodeos in the nation. He wouldn't be alone chasing the average, not this weekend.

"You ready for this?" Carson asked as he patted the horse beneath him. Skeeter just tossed his head, not that Carson noticed. Nothing rattled his brother, probably because he looked upon team roping as a hobby, not a career. It still irked Shane that he'd made it to the NFR without even trying. He'd probably make it again this year, too, thanks in part to their win last night. That irritated the heck out of him, too. He hadn't roped with his brother in months, maybe even a year, and yet the two of them had gone out there like old-time partners, scoring a win and helping Carson get one step closer to the NFR while he had to work his butt off riding bulls.

Figured.

"I'm ready for this to be over," he quipped. Team roping wasn't his favorite sport, much to his father's chagrin.

"You know, we could really make a go of this if you ever wanted to."

Shane looked over at Carson. "I thought you were the one that didn't take roping seriously."

"I don't. I like cutting horses better, but I enjoy making money at it. And we're good together, clearly. I'm just saying, if you ever get tired of riding bulls…"

"Forget it, bro. Bull riding's my thing. Roping is yours…when you feel like it."

His brother just shook his head and looked away. Shane patted his horse, Hotrod, the gelding's neck sweaty beneath the California sunshine. The rodeo grounds were on the fringes of town, not a whole lot of shade to be found. That was okay. He was used to working in the sun. Back at home he ran cattle for his dad or rode horses for the cutting side of the operation. Carson? Not so much. He preferred making things with his hands, and he was good at that, too.

"Just make sure you turn him fast," Carson teased. "*If* you catch."

Shane hardly paid attention to the dig, and it was a dig, because the truth was that Shane had more trouble catching a steer's horns than Carson ever did the heels. Shane liked to say that was because it was easier to catch the back legs, but that wasn't true. Both required skill. The difference was his brother had been born a team roper and Shane hadn't.

She hadn't arrived yet.

The abrupt change of direction of his thoughts took him by surprise until he realized he'd spotted someone standing outside the warm-up area that looked so much like Kait he had had to do a double take. The woman must have noticed his stare because when she caught his eye, she smiled in a provocative manner. She wore a hokey-looking hat, but her hair was the same shade of blond and her figure just as trim. He looked away, and for some reason his cheeks heated up like a kid caught staring at a girlie magazine.

She didn't hold a candle to Kait. His wife. His pregnant wife. A wife he'd had a hell of a time keeping his hands off all week.

"Well, look who's here."

Shane's head whipped around, and he couldn't keep the smile from his face when he spotted her walking toward him. Only she didn't look happy. Neither did her mother and he realized why an instant later when the same woman who'd caught his eye earlier walked up to him, touched his knee and said with a suggestive smile, "Can I have your autograph?"

Damn. Kait had caught him staring at the woman.

"Sure," he said, nodding toward Kait and her mother. "Just as soon as I say hello to my wife."

The woman stepped back in surprise. He all but kicked Hotrod into a gallop. He saw the woman's eyes go wide just before he trotted off. Kait saw him, too, taking a few quick steps back when he pulled his horse up in front of her.

"There you are," he said, hopping off Hotrod before bending down to kiss her.

He saw her eye his horse askance, but then her gaze focused on him, and as always happened, all it took was one look and the chemistry shot between them, and he found himself bending and kissing her before he could think better of it.

"Now, now," said her mom. "Save that for the bedroom, you two."

The bedroom. A place he'd fantasized about all week. But he'd been afraid to touch her, worried that he might harm her in some way if she allowed him to make love to her. But there was another fear, too. He worried she'd turn him away. Only as he kissed her did he realize she wouldn't have done that. They might be near strangers, but there would always be this, the crazy chemistry that made him come alive whenever he kissed her.

She drew back and looked up at him, arching a brow. "Who's your new friend?"

He turned and realized the woman had followed him. She held a straw hat in her hand, a pen in the other one.

"To tell you the truth, I thought it was you at first."

She lifted the other brow.

"Except I should have known you'd never wear a cowboy hat." He tweaked her nose, and he realized in that moment that he was so happy to see her his heart had jumped in excitement.

"Kaitlin Cooper?"

And now it was his turn to lift a brow because it was clear she'd been recognized, too.

"It is you, isn't it?" said a kid who didn't look old enough to drive, much less follow racing. "Wow. I read you were married to a rodeo guy, but I didn't think I'd actually see you here today." The kid turned toward a woman who shot them all a look of apology. "Mom, do you have a piece of paper? I need an autograph. And a picture. Man, Patrick won't believe this."

"I'm so sorry," said the mom dressed in traditional rodeo garb right down to the fancy Western shirt and jeans. "We didn't mean to interrupt."

"Mo-om."

"It's okay," Kait said with a smile. "To tell you the truth, it's flattering to be recognized."

She smiled so kindly at the kid and at the mom that

Shane could only stare. She wasn't like so many celebrities he'd met over the years. Kait was genuine and down to earth, and he decided then and there to hell with it. He wanted Kait in his life. Not just as the mother of his babies. He wanted more. Much more.

"Shane, we gotta go," called his brother still atop his own horse.

Shane waved, turned back to Kait and gave her a quick peck on the cheek. "When I'm done roping today, he'll want my autograph, too."

The blonde woman came forward with her pen in hand. Kait signed an autograph for the boy. And it was a relief to finally admit to himself that he was done fighting it. He wanted her in more than name only.

"Shane," said his brother. "We gotta go, buddy."

He finished writing his name with a flourish, smiled at the blonde beneath the hat, then glanced at his wife.

His wife.

Damn, he liked saying that.

"You should get her autograph, too. She's way more famous than me."

He slapped Kait on the butt, shooting her a flirtatious smile, but as he turned away, he caught a glimpse of her mother's face. She seemed bemused. Or maybe happy. Maybe even a little bit relieved.

He knew exactly how she felt.

Chapter Thirteen

He won.

Kait had watched him back his horse between some fences only to shoot back out a split second later and chase after a baby cow that he somehow managed to rope in a matter of seconds—four and a half, to be exact. And then his brother had done the same thing to the back legs of the cow, and it'd all been over so fast she wished they'd had a replay of it on the big screen. Instead the only thing the big monitor showed was Shane's smiling face and his name above the words *NEW LEADER* that flashed and then exploded like confetti on the screen.

"You weren't kidding when you said he was good." Her mom leaned in next to her, but she still had to raise her voice to be heard over the roar of the crowd.

"And this isn't even his usual event," Kait muttered.

She was tempted, boy was she ever tempted, to go down and congratulate him, but she told herself to stay put. She didn't need to be on her feet more than she had to be. And Shane wouldn't want her down there. He'd be busy getting ready for the bull riding.

Her stomach flipped end over end again.

So strange to be the one sitting in the grandstands.

And yet… She felt pride, too. Shane and Carson ended up winning the team roping. That made it two in a row, something the announcer told the audience of rodeo fans applauding their approval. They watched cowboys try to ride bucking horses next, a few of them getting tossed so high in the air it took her breath away.

Would that happen to Shane?

"You okay?" her mom asked.

Nervous, scared, but most of all troubled that she seemed so emotionally invested in the welfare of a man she barely knew.

"I'm fine."

Bull riding came all too quickly. She tried to spot Shane across the arena behind the bucking chutes. They all looked the same, though, the cowboys with their low-brim hats and shiny chaps painted all different colors. There was no leaderboard to tell her when he'd go or even what chute he'd be in, so she had to sit and wait as one cowboy after another was tossed, trampled and, in one case, run over. It made her ill.

"You look nervous."

"I'm fine," she repeated again, more forcefully this time. She caught a glimpse of her mother's face, how-ever, and she could tell she knew her daughter wasn't "fine."

"Ladies and gentlemen, put your hands together for a local cowboy next. Shane Gillian, four-time NFR qual-ifier and California's leading bull rider, according to the standings."

She felt as though she'd stepped off the edge of a cliff. She'd never experienced anything like it.

Her mom grabbed her hand. One look at her mom's face and she knew she understood.

Why?

Why was she so afraid? It wasn't like they were in love.

He's the father of your babies.

Yes, but that was all he was to her. *Right?*

"Shane will be riding a bull called Lightning Rod today, and let me tell you, ladies and gentlemen, this bull is one of the best. Bred by California's own Four Star Rodeo out of Cottonwood, California. He had an average score of 89, but that's only if he's ridden."

Her fingers must have been cutting off the blood flow to her mother's hand.

"Looks like we're about ready to go. Stomp your feet if you want to watch a local cowboy win."

In the grandstands, hundreds of feet rattled the aluminum slats. It sounded like thunder.

The chute opened. Kait gasped because the bull didn't wait to buck. He came out front feet in the air, Shane clinging to his back. She covered her mouth with her hands and stood, watching Shane cling to the animal's back as it bucked and bucked and bucked, turning this way and that, Shane's hand up in the air, his legs moving. Spurring, that was what he'd called it. He spurred the animal on.

She sank back down on her seat.

She'd never seen anything so exhilarating in her life. Not even when she'd watched the open-wheel cars in Europe last year. That was just a few seconds of cars passing in front of their spectators' box followed by long pauses until it happened again. This went on and on and on, or so it seemed. The buzzer sounded, but Shane was already flying off, as if he'd known in his head how long he needed to ride, and he probably did.

"Ladies and gentlemen," the announcer cried. "How about *that* for a bull ride?"

More feet stomped. People yelled. Someone cried out, "We love you, Shane," and Kait just sat there, stunned.

"That was amazing," her mom said. "I can't see how anyone could possible beat that."

Kait agreed.

Her mom would be proven right. They would watch four more bull riders, but none of them would come close to matching Shane's score of ninety-one.

When it was over, she told herself she didn't need to see him. She could send him a text message. Tell him she'd been feeling ill. She didn't need him to know how exhilarating she'd found it watching him compete.

"Don't you want to go down and congratulate him?"

"We don't need to do that." She held up her hand and the stamp someone had placed on the back of it. "I don't want to get in the way."

"He's your husband, Kait. It might look strange if you don't."

Her mom had a point. But if she were honest with herself, she wanted to see him. It dawned on her then that she'd never really been with a man who was competitive in a sport. She'd always been the one running off to a racetrack somewhere in America. So it was a unique experience to be the one on the sidelines, cheering someone on.

Cheering a sexy someone on.

She shoved that thought away with a mental thrust of willpower. The place was packed, and she and her mom had to duck and dodge people with drinks in their hands and little kids running ahead of harried parents.

She was almost relieved when they pushed through the crowd, having to go all the way around to get to exhibitor parking area. Then it was like trying to find a needle in a haystack. All the trucks and trailers looked alike. She'd seen the Gillian Ranch trailer parked in front of the stables and incorrectly assumed it would be easy to find.

"At this rate we might need to ambush that guy on his golf cart." Her mom shot her a worried glance. "Maybe you should sit down for a minute."

"There it is," she said, relieved, the logo of their ranch clearly visible on the side of a trailer as big as a house. He hadn't seen her. He was busy taking care of his horse, had removed the saddle, the horse's back wet with sweat. He was hanging something up. Hay, she realized, and his brother was off to the side talking to a pretty girl.

"Congratulations," her mom said, which drew Shane's attention and she watched as his eyes sparked with happiness when he spotted them. "Kait told me you were good, but I had no idea how good until just now."

"I got lucky," he said, quickly finishing his task. "Drew a good bull."

Humility. He had it in spades. It was something she'd noticed about him before.

"You weren't lucky." Kait hung back a little. Truth be told, she felt out of place. This was his world not hers, and it was strange to be the odd man out. Plus she was afraid of horses, something she had yet to share with Shane.

"Thanks," he said, and she wondered if he'd come over to her again and kiss her senseless like he had earlier. She could still feel where his lips had touched her own, but he didn't move from the side of her horse. "Come on over and meet Hotrod."

Her mom snorted. Kait shot her a look. Her fear of large animals was well known in the Cooper family.

"I'm kind of tired." She smiled back. "I just wanted to say congratulations before we head back home."

"You're leaving?"

She nodded. "I don't want to overdo it."

"You can't leave now. I thought we could go to dinner."

"We already ate."

"We did," her mom said. "Sorry. It's been forever since I had a corndog. But I think you and Kait should ride home together."

What?

Her mom smiled at her before nodding. "He's always so busy back at the ranch. Spend some time together."

"It wouldn't be just the two of us," Kait said quickly. "His brother will be with us."

"No, he won't." Shane shot his brother a wry smile. Carson still stood talking to the two girls. "He's catching a ride back home with someone else. Wants to stick around for the dance tonight."

Kait didn't want to do it, though. Yes, she'd hated how he'd kept his distance all week, but she'd told herself that was for the best. And, yes, she'd had the odd thought or two that maybe their marriage could turn into something more real, but that had been a brief lapse in sanity.

It's just a drive home.

She glanced at her mom, who smiled at her secretively. She knew what her mom was trying to do. Knew this was her way of forcing them together. Knew her mom hoped they could work things out, too, but there was so much more to it than that. Yes, she could no longer deny the chemistry between her and Shane. A week of him sleeping on the couch had taught her that. But it took so much more than sexual attraction to make a relationship work. They both had high-profile careers. How in the hell could they have a meaningful relationship if one of them was always jetting off somewhere? Her job required her to be at a racetrack four days a week, two of those on the weekend. His job required him to compete on the weekends, too. So that left them what? Three days together? Impossible.

"Go on," said her mom, shooing her with her hands. "Drive home with your husband. I insist. Wanted to do a little sightseeing while I was here, anyway. I'll just do it today."

No. No, no, no.

She pleaded with her eyes, but her mom just shook her head, and she knew that Cooper stubbornness well. Her mom had made up her mind and there'd be no changing it. For whatever reason, she wanted her to spend more time with her husband.

A husband who didn't want her.

"I'll go sit inside the truck."

IT DIDN'T TAKE him long to load up the horses. Carson helped out, just as soon as he'd torn himself away from the women he'd been trying to charm the pants off of...literally.

The gold of his wedding ring caught the glint of the sun as he set his hands on the steering wheel and turned toward his wife. To be honest, he half expected Kait to be asleep and he was surprised when she turned and said, "I can rent a car if you don't want to be with me."

"What?"

She couldn't be serious. He shook his head. "Why in the heck would I want you to do that?"

"I don't know. I just thought…"

He started up the truck, the big diesel vehicle rumbled to life and he let it idle while he waited for an answer. "You just thought what?"

She pushed her lips together in obvious disgruntlement. "I just thought you might want to keep on avoiding me like you've done all week."

So that was it? It'd bothered her that he'd kept his distance.

I'll be damned.

He put the truck in gear, careful to avoid hitting a steer wrestler who waved at him as he pulled out. Everyone knew everyone on the rodeo circuit and so he smiled and waved back before saying to Kait, "I wasn't avoiding you. I was trying to give you space."

Did she have any idea how hard it'd been to keep away from her? How difficult it'd been to stay on that damn uncomfortable couch? And right now? For him to not reach out and touch her? With her hair loose around her shoulders and that gauzy off-white blouse thing she wore, she looked like something out of a Western-living magazine.

"You gave me space all right," she mumbled.

He bit back a smile. He had to force himself to concentrate on getting out of the rodeo grounds without running over an exhibitor or spectator. That was good, too, because something about her words had him feeling hopeful. It gave him the courage to say what was on his mind, even though it was a full five minutes later before he had what he wanted to say all worked out.

"I think we should make this a real marriage."

She turned to face him so fast her hair fluffed out. "Excuse me?"

"You know…" And still he fumbled for the right words. "We should turn this into a real relationship. The whole nine yards. The full Monty."

Her stare was the unblinking kind. "Did my mom put you up to this?"

He pulled his gaze away from the road so he could shoot her a frown. "No."

It was a relief when she turned away to stare out the front windshield. She didn't seem all that happy to be having the conversation, though, and that gave him pause.

"Okay, look. I'm going to be completely honest," she said, half turning toward him. "I've been thinking that maybe we should go our separate ways."

He flinched.

"Permanently. After the babies are born and we figure out all the custody issues."

"What?"

She nodded. "I've done the math, Shane. My race schedule plus your rodeo schedule plus travel time to your place in California and my place in North Carolina." She pinned him with a stare. "And I've come to a conclusion."

He could see what it was in her eyes.

"There is no way we could ever make this work, not without dragging our kids all over kingdom come."

"Yeah, but, we're making it work right now."

"Because I've been grounded. What about after the

babies are born? Will you follow me to North Carolina? Because if you don't, you'll barely see the babies. And I can't move to California. So how would it work?"

He got that. He'd been racking his brain all week about how to solve the same problem. It would mean uprooting his whole life. Changing his game plan.

Severing ties with his dad.

His old man would never forgive him if he took off to parts unknown. He would look at it as a serious step backward, even though there was no reason why he couldn't continue bull riding from the East Coast. The horses and the roping and riding cutting horses? That would go by the wayside unless he found a job somewhere doing the same. But he could make it work, even though he could practically hear his father's voice.

Leave your family? For a woman?

"Look," he said, "we're good together. I think if there's a chance we can make this work for real, we should give it a try."

She finally stopped shaking her head, but only so she could look directly at him. "It'll never work out."

"Not with that attitude, it won't."

She released a sigh of exasperation. "Do you know how many marriages I've seen fail in the racing industry? Good marriages. Solid ones. And they didn't fail because someone cheated or they grew apart. I've lost track of how many times I've been told it's the business we're in. It sucks the life out of you, and I'm one of the lucky ones. I work for my family. I don't have the added burden of always wondering if I'll have a job next season. It's the time, Shane. Always on the road. Always flying around the country. Always making an appearance somewhere. Never at home. Plus…" She looked out the window for a second. When she met his gaze again he could see the seriousness in her eyes. "…I don't want to be separated from my babies. I think they should live with me, and I know that's a big thing to ask, but you can visit them whenever you want. I'd make it as easy on you as possible, and more importantly, I think it'd be better for the kids. My race schedule is crazy, but plenty of drivers bring their children with them. There's even a mobile day care center at the track. And I'll be on the West Coast often enough that'd it'd be easy for you to visit. We could work it out."

It felt like she hit him. "You mean you don't want to share custody?"

"No. I mean, you'll see them. I just think I should be the primary care giver."

"So what were you expecting me to do?" he asked. "Play it by ear on when I can see my kids?"

"Something like that."

He'd never felt more disheartened in his life. He'd thought they'd had a shot. After a week of sleeping on the couch and wishing like hell he could just go to her, he'd hoped there was something there. To hell with that. He *knew* they had a connection. But she wanted to push it aside. To ignore it. To take on the burden of having the babies live with her while he…what? Became a part-time father? Not on his life.

"I'll think about it," he said.

But he wasn't going to think about it in the way she wanted. No. He'd just have to work harder to bring her to his way of thinking. The rest of it, well, they'd find some way to work it all out.

There were some things that were worth fighting for.

Chapter Fourteen

They arrived back home as the sun was setting, Kait having stayed awake the whole ride home, which had her hoping maybe the days of always wanting to sleep were behind her. They hadn't talked a whole lot, but that wasn't surprising given the bombshell she'd dropped.

"I can stop at the house before I head to the barn, if you want," he said.

"No. That's okay." She didn't want to be a burden. She already felt like one of those.

"I just need to unload the horses. Shouldn't take me more than a few minutes."

She nodded, admiring the way the sun lit the tops of the oak trees in the same way it did the edges of a cloud. The angle of the sun painted the valley where his family's ranch sat a vibrant gold. Sometimes the rolling hills reminded her of the Smoky Mountains. It should have soothed her homesick soul, but it didn't. Not even the pretty sight of the ranch with the red tile roofs lit up this time of day could capture her attention.

"You know what? I think I'm just going to walk back to the house."

The little house they shared with its white picket fence and fragrant flowers that she'd grown fond of after only a week. After the babies were born, she'd have to leave it. She wondered how long she'd have to wait. Would it look bad if she left right away?

"Actually, hang on and I'll walk back with you."

"No. That's okay." She didn't want to be near him for some reason. "You don't need to do that."

"But I want to," he said. "Just hang tight. I'll be right back."

She wanted to tell him no again, but she'd already hurt his feelings once tonight. It couldn't have been easy to hear her say she wanted primary custody of their children. She'd hated to suggest it, but it really would be better for the kids.

Easier for you.

Because she didn't want him to know how hard it'd been to turn down his offer of a "real" marriage. As much as she'd been tempted she just couldn't do it to them both. The man had no idea what he was up against. She'd seen the damage a racing career could do to other couples. And then their kids…it would end up hurting them in the end, too. No. She truly felt she'd made the right choice. She just needed to get him to see things her way. .

So she stood in the cool evening air, a rooster crowing in the distance, a horse neighing in welcome inside the barn. It didn't take him long to unload first one horse and then the other, but he paused by the end of the truck with that second horse.

"I don't think you've ever met Hotrod."

She frowned because she didn't want to, either.

"Hi, Hotrod," she said with a forced smile.

"Come on over and pet him."

"No."

Beneath his cowboy hat his eyes grew puzzled. "You wouldn't greet him at the rodeo, either."

"I just prefer to keep my distance."

"Why? He won't bite."

"Just the same, I'll pass."

The narrowed eyes suddenly went wide. "Are you afraid of horses?"

"No," she instantly lied. "I just have a healthy respect for them."

"No way."

"I'm not afraid."

"You are, too."

"No, I'm not."

"Kaitlin Cooper. The darling of the racing world. A woman who drives a car two hundred miles per hour and she's afraid of my wittle pony?"

"He's hardly a pony."

"Actually, he is pretty short for a horse."

Her cheeks had begun to warm in embarrassment. "Size doesn't matter."

"Come here."

She hated being bossed around, she really did. She thought about turning and simply walking away, but he'd only see that as proof of his point, and for some strange reason she didn't want him to know just how terrified she was of the animals.

She took a deep breath because Shane was right. She handled hundreds of horsepower. This was just one little animal.

With big feet. And really big teeth.

"Give me your hand," Shane said when she reluctantly moved forward. The horse ignored her. He was busy staring at the barn as if silently contemplating making a break for it. She took Shane's hand and when she did, all her fear faded away and she really hated how that happened. One touch and it was just her and him. She very nearly forgot about the big animal nearby. Well, almost.

"Come on. Touch his muzzle." He drew her hand up to the horse's mouth, and she felt her heart begin to race. "It's the softest part of a horse."

"I really don't want—"

The horse snorted.

She jumped, turned. Shane caught her and then he laughed and stared down at her, and there it was again, the burn in the pit of her belly.

"You really don't like them, do you?"

"No," she admitted.

Something began to change in his eyes, and her whole body warmed. His smile turned tender and it did the same thing to her that it always did. It turned her insides into mush. Most men stared at her like they hadn't had a meal in weeks. Either that or like she might bite them. Some men didn't know how to act around her. They were either too overbearing or too aloof. Shane had never had that problem. Around her he was just… himself.

"You are the strangest woman I've ever met."

"Thanks."

"And I'm going to kiss you."

"Shane, I don't think—"

"Shhh." He pressed a finger against her mouth.

"But—"

"You think too much."

And then he kissed her and she melted into him because that was what always happened whenever their lips touched and it just wasn't fair. Damn it. Why did he have to be Shane Gillian, famous bull rider with a career as demanding as hers? And why did she have to be Kaitlin Cooper, daughter of the famous Lance Cooper, born with racing in her blood. And then she admitted he was right. She thought too much.

He only had one free hand and he somehow managed to slip it beneath her blouse. This, what he did to her at that moment, that was what she'd been missing at night as she'd lain awake, waiting...hoping.

He pulled his lips away, but only so he could nip the side of her neck, and she moaned because it felt *so good.*

"I want to take you to my bed."

Her body reacted to his words in a way she'd never felt before. Every nerve ending fired. Her body warmed. She could feel the effect of his touch all the way to her toes.

"I've been dreaming about it all week."

He had? Why hadn't he done something about it then?

You should be grateful he kept his distance.

She'd never been more conflicted in her life. She wanted him. She even tipped her head to the side so he could keep nibbling and licking her. And when his hand found her breast, she arched into him. She wanted him, but she should stop him. This wouldn't make things any easier.

"Kait," he gently whispered in her ear before his mouth caught her lobe, tugging on it, teasing it.

She was going to combust right there. Out in the wide-open field. With his big horse standing nearby.

His palm found her breast again, and she arched into him. He knew exactly how to touch her, this man.

Knew what to say to her, too, because he whispered in her ear all the naughty things he'd like to do to her, and she kept slipping farther and farther downstream, sliding through the eddies, letting her body go.

"Let's go back home."

Home. The word jolted her back to reality. This wasn't her home. It would never be her home. And he wasn't her husband. Well, not really. In name only.

She stepped back. "I can't."

He stared down at her, puzzled, his horse tossing its head as if agreeing with his question.

"Please don't kiss me again." She saw his face fill with disbelief, so she quickly added, "Not until we have this all figured out. We're only making things more difficult."

"Kait—"

"No." She turned, waving a hand at him. "We can talk in the morning."

"Why not now?"

Because she was too conflicted. Because when he touched her, she didn't know which way was up, much less down...or what to think about a future with him. Because for the first time in her life, she felt herself falling for someone.

And it scared her to death.

IF HE'D BEEN the physical type he would have punched a hole in the stable wall. His horse seemed to sense his mood, all but trotting away from him when he turned him loose in his stall.

"Son of a—"

"I heard you won tonight."

He straightened. Just what he needed, damn it. Dad.

He turned, closed the stall door, took a deep breath before facing his father. "Won both events. I had to head for Carson, too."

His father just stared. No word of praise. No clap on the back. No "attaboy." He should be used to it by now, but it always stung.

"Saw you out there with your wife."

Was there an emphasis on the word *wife*? It sure sounded like it.

"She must be good luck," Shane said, turning back to the stall to make sure the latch was secure. Hotrod moved around inside, sniffing the ground, the disturbance of his passing sending the scent of pine shavings through the air. He was going to roll.

"Son, what are you doing?"

He'd been expecting this conversation. All week long he'd waited. They'd bumped into each other more than once, but his dad had ignored him.

"I'm trying to do the right thing, Dad. That's what."

He crossed his arms in front of himself, his stance wide, and faced off with his dad in a way he didn't normally do. Carson was the one who was always mouthing off. His little brother didn't give a damn what their father thought about his actions. Shane did. From the time he'd been five years old, he'd wanted to be just like him. Famous in the rodeo world. He'd started off team roping, but it quickly became apparent he didn't have his father's roping chops. But bull riding? That was what he was good at, and his father had never disapproved of anything he'd done. Until now.

"Do you love her?"

The question took him aback. "I care for her." He tipped his chin. "She's the mother of my unborn babies."

"Yeah, twins."

He hadn't told his dad. He assumed Crystal had spilled the beans. She'd been overjoyed by the news, as had his siblings and cousins.

"I'm thinking about moving to North Carolina."

"When?"

"Not right away."

"You know I need your help with that big cutting show we have coming up."

"I know that."

His dad's gray brows lifted. "So once your kids are born then?"

He could see his dad getting more and more irate as the reality of what he'd said sunk in.

"Maybe before then. I don't know."

He recognized the signs of his dad's burgeoning temper well. The ticking jaw muscle. The blood rushing to his neck. The eyes narrowing.

"So you're going to give it all up, then."

"No, Dad." Shane unfolded his arms. "I'm not going to give it all up. I'd just be relocating."

"Away from your family."

That would be hard. He wouldn't deny it.

"Away from the people who've supported you for your entire career."

"Dad, it's not like I'm traveling to the moon."

"Where will you live?"

"With Kait."

His dad shook his head. "And she's just going to let you move in. You think you're going to compete like you always do, going to rodeos while she stays home and does what, Shane? Bake cookies and take care of those babies? Because you know that's not going to happen."

Shane turned away for a moment. His dad had a way of making his own anger flare.

"No," he said when he'd calmed himself. "It won't be like that. She'd still race. I'll still ride. We'd both take care of the babies."

His dad's snort of derision startled a horse in a nearby stall. "You're in complete denial."

"No, I'm not."

"Why do you think I was so angry that day you came home with her?"

"*What* are you talking about?"

His dad took his hat off, swiped the little bit of gray hair he had left back off his head. "She's a big celebrity, Shane. Yes, even I recognized her that first day. What the hell are you thinking getting involved with her?"

"Dad, it's not like I planned this."

"You'll never have your own life if you get together with her. Sure, do your duty by your kids, that can't be avoided, but don't go running off to North Carolina like you're some kind of groupie."

"Dad," he said again, trying to hold on to his own temper. "It's not like that."

"No?" The brows swooped down. "Maybe not at first, but it'll happen sooner or later. And what of your own career? You're at the point where you're finally starting to attract attention. You've got new sponsors. That big magazine spread coming out in a few weeks. The TV deal. You're focused and ready to go. At least, you were. You could have won the whole shebang this year. Hell, if you keep pairing up with your brother, you might even be in line for an all-around."

"Did I miss something?" Shane had to work to keep his voice level. "Because I'm pretty sure I won a huge chunk of change today."

"Won't matter."

Shane just about lost it then. His old man held up a hand. "Hear me out, son. Now you've got this woman, and she's not even some buckle bunny that you can tuck away back home. No. She's a big famous race-car driver with a career that'll take her here, there and everywhere…and you with her. Before you know it, she'll expect you to be at her races. She'll be making demands. You'll be torn between a rock and a hard spot and not concentrating on your own career. The sponsors will go away. The money will go away, and you can bet your ass you can kiss your shot at winning the average at the finals goodbye. You're not getting any younger. Hell, most bull riders your age have already retired."

So what, Shane wanted to say. *So frickin' what.* He'd just turned thirty, but he was in the best shape of his life. Why didn't his dad believe in him?

"Bull riding will always be there for me," he said even as a part of him knew his father was right. His days were numbered, but he wasn't over the hill just yet. "So what if my plans shift and I don't win any big titles right away It'd be a sacrifice for sure, but it'd be worth it. I already stepped away once before…for mom."

He didn't mean to get under his dad's skin. He could tell the words were a direct hit, though.

"Someone had to keep making money."

That had always been his dad's excuse for letting Shane bear the brunt of his mom's illness. At first it'd been no big deal. They'd thought his mom had the flu. To this day he had no idea why it'd taken the doctors so long to diagnose her illness, but through it all his dad had been away from home.

"I know that," Shane said, taking another deep breath. Experience had taught him that you never got far with his dad by losing your temper. "The point is that I don't mind stepping away from things if that's what needs to be done."

"For how long?"

Shane shrugged.

"You're not getting any younger, son. You should have won at least a few world titles by now. Instead, all you've done is win a few rounds here and there. You can't afford to sit it out."

His dad said it like winning a round at the finals meant nothing, but it did mean something. A lot of guys would kill to be in his boots. And this year, he'd been so close to winning it all—that coveted gold buckle his dad wanted so much for him—but did that mean anything to his dad? No.

Okay, calm down.

"I appreciate your concern, but I know what I'm doing."

His dad just shook his head. "I sure hope you do."

But as his dad walked away, he wondered if he did.

Chapter Fifteen

Shane didn't come back right away. That surprised Kait, but she appreciated the space he gave her.

He wasn't home by the time she slipped into bed, either. She woke up at midnight to a completely quiet house, and even though she told herself not to, she slipped out of bed, peeked through a crack in her door. The place was small enough that she had a direct view of the couch.

Empty.

She turned away and leaned back on the door, telling herself she should be grateful. He was honoring her wishes and keeping his distance until they sorted everything out. Still, as she crawled back between the sheets, she wondered where he was. Ironic that for someone who couldn't seem to stay away, she suddenly found herself unable to sleep. She must have drifted off at some point because when she next opened her eyes, the sun shone through her window. Another beautiful California day. She was beginning to think it never rained.

He hadn't come home.

She knew it the moment she opened the bedroom door—fully dressed, just in case—the pillow on the couch in the exact same place it'd been when she'd peeked through the door last night.

You should text him. Maybe something happened.

But she knew that wasn't true. She would bet he'd slept in the old bunkhouse with his brothers. Had probably told them some story about the two of them having a fight. Was probably there right now, eating breakfast with his family while she wanted to…

Cry.

Damn this pregnancy and my swinging emotions, she thought, wiping at the sudden tears in her eyes. It shouldn't matter where he was or who he was with. This wasn't a real marriage.

But it did matter. Terribly. And her vivid imagination wondered if maybe he'd gone into town last night. If maybe he'd hooked up with someone a little more willing.

Her day went from bad to worse when her mom came over.

"I've decided to fly home."

Kait stared into her mom's blue eyes and wanted to scream, "Nooooo." They sat in the small kitchen her mom had furnished in a Southwestern style, right down to the hanging pack of red peppers above the stove.

"Your dad called this morning and begged me to come back." She played with a cactus-shaped salt-and-pepper shaker. "Seems he can't live more than a few days apart from me."

And that depressed Kait all the more. What would it be like to have a marriage like her mom and dad's? She'd probably never know.

"Are you okay?" Her mom's head tilted, her long

red hair falling around her shoulders. "Has the cramping started again?"

"No. It's not that." She actually felt better, physically at least, than she ever had. Her heart... Well, that was another matter entirely.

"Is it you and Shane?"

"We're fine," Kait said. She stood and went to the refrigerator, which was made to look like something from the '50s but was actually modern on the inside. "Didn't sleep very well."

She came back to the table with a plate of green grapes. Her mom stared at her in concern.

"I hope he's not mad I forced the two of you to drive home together."

"He's not, Mom. It has nothing to do with that at all."

She popped a grape in her mouth, enjoying the sweet taste of it, but when she rested her hand on the table, her mom covered it with her own.

"It'll all work out."

There she went wanting to cry again. Goodness gracious. Would it ever stop? She hated what an emotional wreck she'd become since she'd found out she was pregnant.

"I told him I want to keep the babies with me. That I'm going to keep them with me when I race and that I don't want them to be torn between two households."

Her mom leaned back, her hand sliding from Kait's. She took a grape, too, and Kait heard it burst in her mom's mouth in the dead silence of the kitchen.

"I imagine he didn't take that very well. That man isn't the type to shirk responsibility and he'll look at anything less than raising your twins together as not doing his duty."

Kait tilted her head. "You like him, don't you?"

Her mom nodded. "I think he's the best thing to ever happen to you."

Kait's hand froze midway to the grape bowl.

"You're finally learning there's more to life than driving race cars."

"What do you mean?"

Her mom's eyes filled with an emotion Kait couldn't quite pinpoint. "I've watched you for a lot of years, first in go-karts and then dirt tracks. You and your brother, always racing, and I was fine with that. I might have wanted something different for you than racing, but you were a pioneer, and so I put my own concerns aside."

"What concerns?"

"Getting killed."

She drew back. They never talked about that. Never mentioned the dreaded *D* word.

Death.

"Kait, listen. You've opened doors you probably don't even know you've opened. Little girls around the world want to be you, and that's a good thing, don't get me wrong, but I'd be lying if I said I've enjoyed every minute of it."

She could see it all in her mom's eyes: pride. Approval. But also fear and sadness.

"Bad enough I had to watch my husband defy death all those years. Now I have to watch you and Jarrod."

She and her brother were rivals on the track, but not in life. He was the one she could always count on when she got in a tight spot on the track.

"You have to think about that now, Kait. You're going to be a mother. You have two little lives growing inside of you. Maybe giving you twins was God's way of saying slow down."

Everything inside her froze. "You think I should give up racing?"

Her mom captured her hands. Both of them this time. "I think you should do what's best for the babies."

Give it up. Walk away from the sport she loved. Don't risk her life when she had two other lives depending on her.

"I don't know what to do, Mom."

She was crying and she didn't even know it. That was what pregnancy did to you. Turned you into a water pot.

Her mom came around the table, bent and wrapped her arms around her. "You'll figure it out."

Yes, but not with her mom by her side. She admitted then how much she'd come to count on her.

"You're leaving because you want to push me and Shane together."

Her mom drew back. Kait wiped at her eyes so she could see her better.

"I'm leaving because I did you a terrible disservice. Had I not been here, maybe you and Shane would have become closer."

"Actually, Mom, I don't know what I would have done without you."

Now her mom looked close to tears. "Come here."

They hugged, Kait inhaling the familiar scent that could only be her mother. How she loved her. And now she understood just what it was like to watch someone you love…

She drew back.

"What is it?" her mom asked.

She didn't love Shane. There was no way. That was crazy.

"I just remembered I have a doctor's appointment today."

"I know. I set a reminder. I already sent Shane a text message. He'll take you."

Love was too strong a word. Admiration. She admired him. Like a really good friend. And watching him ride yesterday had been terrifying. Funny that she'd never felt that kind of deep-in-the-gut terror when watching her dad or her brother drive. Just Shane.

"He probably planned on taking me, anyway. He's been great about this."

Her mom swiped a lock of hair away from Kait's cheek. "That man cares for you, honey. More than you know. I can see it in his eyes."

She could see it, too.

"You just need to figure out what you're going to do about it," her mom said before bending to kiss her goodbye.

"EVERYTHING LOOKS GOOD."

Shane felt his whole body go slack at the words.

The doctor's smile encompassed them both, the glasses on his nose bobbing up as he smiled. "Strong heartbeats. Normal growth rate. Uterus looks good, too. You said your cramping is gone?"

From her position on the doctor's table, Kait nodded. "I'm actually feeling a lot better."

"Good," the doctor said, helping her sit up after he pulled her shirt down. "I don't see any reason why you can't resume some of your usual activities. I still don't want you on your feet a lot. And no more traveling to rodeos." He wagged a finger in her face. "I still can't believe you did that."

"Got it. Sorry." She rearranged her pink T-shirt. "I just thought since I'd be sitting in a car…"

"It's not about the sitting. It's about getting you the care you need if something goes wrong. No more traveling."

She looked crushed. Shane wondered just how soon she'd planned to go home. After her mom's surprise departure, he'd wondered if she would follow, but it looked like that wouldn't happen.

Thank God.

He'd done a lot of thinking last night while sleeping in the bunkhouse in his old bed, his brothers and cousins snoring nearly as loudly as Kait did. His dad was right. Kait was right, too. He shouldn't kiss her again. He was crazy to think the two of them could have a life together, so even though he wanted to push her to see what happened, he would keep his distance from here on out.

"I would say we're good for a due date of September 1, barring any unforeseen circumstances," said the doctor. "They might come a little earlier than that. With twins, you never know."

"September," Kait repeated, as if that news surprised her.

"In the meantime, make sure to eat healthy and get plenty of rest."

Shane stepped forward. "We have a big event coming up at the ranch. Cutting show. I was thinking maybe Kait would like to help out. Work the office. Maybe hand out prizes. Would that be okay?"

Kait looked at him in surprise. Might was well keep busy until she left.

"I don't see why not." The doctor's kindly face lifted into a smile. "Good for her to be out-of-doors."

They talked for a little longer. When it came time to leave, Shane helped Kait up, the two of them walking into the bright Via Del Caballo sunshine.

"You don't have to help with our horse show if you don't want to," he said. "I just thought you might enjoy having something to do."

"No. That sounds interesting. As long as I don't have to get too near the animals."

The words brought to mind their kiss and how hard it'd been not to run after her when she'd walked away. "I promise. There's plenty to do without having to touch a horse." It was the most they'd spoken since he'd picked her up this morning. She'd been quiet, but then, so had he…and he hated it. He hated the whole damn situation.

"I still can't believe you're afraid of horses."

She slipped into his truck. He closed the door for her before moving around to his side.

"Don't confuse respect with being afraid."

He shot her a smile meant to convey without words that he wasn't buying it. "Anything else you're afraid of?"

She just shook her head.

"Spiders."

That got her to turn around and look at him with derision in her eyes.

"Mice?"

She just rolled her eyes. She turned and went back to staring out the front window.

"Winnie the Pooh?"

Her lips twitched.

"I hear that's a thing."

It was as if her cheeks were in a battle of tug-of-war with her sense of humor. Up, down. Up, down. Until, at last, her sense of humor won out, but she turned away before he could see her smile.

Why couldn't it always be like this? he wondered. Why couldn't she be a regular woman with a normal job? How different would things have been if they'd started dating after that first night in Vegas? Things might have turned out so differently.

It was a thought that repeated itself over the next week as, true to his word, he kept his distance. Nobody said anything when he went back to living in the bunkhouse. It wasn't as if the paparazzi lurked in the bushes, outing Kait and their fake marriage. She'd told him that so far the racing community hadn't seemed to care about her marriage and pregnancy. Her dad quickly hired a new driver. They'd farmed out her workload. Their media person had spun her absence like some kind of romantic movie. Love at first sight. So for the most part, everything had been smoothed over. Professionally, at least.

But she missed being in North Carolina. He could see the longing in her eyes when he went to go check on her—which was daily—and asked her about her family. He wondered how he would take it if he'd been told he couldn't ride for nearly a year. He supposed it would have crushed his spirit, too.

So perhaps he shouldn't have been surprised when she threw herself into helping out with the cutting horse competition. His aunt Crystal had always been in charge of managing the ranch's horse shows, the biggest of which was their upcoming Spring Fling. Kait quickly became invaluable to his aunt, or so he'd heard, helping to coordinate entries and personnel and doing the data entry.

"I don't know what I'd do without her," Crystal said a couple days before the show was due to start. People would begin arriving on Tuesday. Down in the valley beneath his dad's place, they'd erected portable stalls near the barn. Their canvas tops looked like strips of tape from a distance. "You sure you can't persuade her to stick around?"

I wish.

He frowned. "She'll be leaving just as soon as the doctor gives her clearance to fly."

They were out on the back veranda. Another Sunday dinner. Kait stood off to the side, talking to his sister, Jayden. His brothers were gathered around the table where they would eat. The smell of barbecue hung in the air, potent at times as smoke billowed in their direction.

"I can't imagine you'll be happy to see her go."

It had dawned an overcast day. They'd almost moved the gathering inside, but the clouds were as patchy as his favorite paint horse. Every once in awhile, sun would pour down, heating the outdoors and making the temperature tolerable. Down in the valley, bright patches of light chased after dark blobs, occasionally illuminating the stable and the outdoor arena and turning the pastures an emerald green.

"Not much I can do about it."

Crystal shook her head. "And I'm sure your dad told you it was all for the best, Kait leaving and all."

It was no secret that his aunt disapproved of his dad in a lot of ways. She'd never forgiven him for deserting his mom when she got so sick. His dad had always put his business first and his family second, something that went against his aunt's grain.

"You know my dad," was all he said.

"Yes," Crystal said, her voice full of derision. "I do."

Kait angled her body to look at something in the backyard that Jayden pointed out, and he could see what she tried hard to hide. The smallest of bulges. Not enough that she had to wear special clothes, but it was there. His babies. *Their* babies.

"Well, forgive me if I have a different opinion. I happen to believe anything can be worked out—if two people care enough."

If they care enough.

Those were the operational words.

His aunt touched his arm. "You do care, don't you?"

He met her gaze. "Of course I do."

Crystal frowned. "Not like that. I mean, do you love her?"

The question was the same one his dad had asked, but for some reason Crystal asking it didn't set his back up.

"We really don't know each other well enough to be in love."

"And why is that?" his aunt asked. "Why haven't you tried to spend more time with her? I know you've been staying at the bunkhouse, the whole ranch knows, and that you try to avoid her whenever possible. That's not exactly conducive to a good relationship."

And his aunt looked so disappointed in him he immediately went on the defensive. "It is what it is. She asked for space, I'm giving it to her."

"And you let her order you around."

"Well," he huffed, "I don't want to make her angry."

His aunt stepped in front of him, her eyes intensely serious. She grabbed his arm, forcing him to look down at her.

"Listen, Shane. I'd like to think your mom would tell you the same thing I'm about to tell you if she were here." She half-turned toward Kait, probably to make sure she wasn't listening. "Don't let her get away. She's a good one. And I don't need to spend a bunch of time with her to know that. Been a big help to me this week. I didn't expect that. With her pedigree and her fame I thought she'd pretend to help or get confrontational when I pushed too hard. She hasn't. She's as kindhearted as she is hardworking. Probably how she got to the top of her profession. Sure she drives race cars and leads a busy life, but so what? You can make it work." She squeezed his arm. "You'll never find another one like her, Shane, believe me. Plus she's the mother of your babies. Go after her. Make her see things your way. If you don't, I'll be disappointed in you."

Having said her piece, Crystal gave one last nod and walked away. Shane watched her go, feeling as if his world had been tipped on end.

His aunt liked her. It amazed him how much weight that carried with him.

But she didn't understand. Kait was the one who'd called a halt to things. He had a feeling when she made up her mind to do something, she did it. And they weren't in love, so it wasn't like there was much holding her here once she got the all clear to go home.

Right?

He felt his stomach flip in the same way his world had flipped because the simple truth was—as he watched her turn to greet his aunt, a smile on her face, long hair hanging loose—he realized he'd been kidding himself these past few days. There was so more between them than just chemistry.

He just wished he knew what to do about it.

Chapter Sixteen

The smell of food woke her up. At first she thought it was her mom she heard in the kitchen, come to make her breakfast, but then she remembered her mom had gone home.

Her eyes sprang open.

It was early morning, not dawn, later than that. Sunshine streamed into her room, and she realized she'd slept far later than she'd thought.

Bacon.

The smell of it made her stomach grumble. She'd been craving it lately. That and fast-food hamburgers. She had no idea why.

A few minutes later, she peeked through a crack in the door and confirmed it was Shane and that he must have the hearing of a bat, because he instantly turned and spotted her staring at him.

"Good morning, sleepyhead," he said with a smile. "Thought you might like some breakfast."

She stood there for a moment absorbing the realization that he was standing in the kitchen stirring something in a pan. Eggs, she realized.

"Come on," he said with a wave of the spatula. "Sit down and eat."

She'd had people do things for her in the past, but she was jaded enough to wonder if they did it for her or in the hopes that she could do something for them. She'd watched it happen with enough times with her famous father that it made her wary. But this…this was all for her, and their babies, she supposed.

"You didn't have to."

"But I wanted to."

Even after she'd told him she'd be leaving. When she'd insisted she would raise their babies. When she'd demanded he stay away from her.

"Thank you."

He just waved her toward the table, where he'd put out the plates her mom had bought. She was so famished that she didn't hesitate. When he pulled out a chair for her, she softened even more. When he scooped an omelet on her plate, one oozing with spinach and cheese, her mouth watered.

"Milk or orange juice?" he asked.

"Juice," she said, her eyes closing when she took her first mouthful. "Delicious."

"Good."

He didn't try to talk to her, just continued cooking. He heaped some bacon on her plate next.

Heaven. She hadn't realized how hungry she was until she sat there eating. When he finished cooking, an omelet and bacon on his own plate, he took a seat opposite her. She ate so fast it wouldn't surprise her if she got a stomachache.

"This is great."

He paused with a forkful halfway to his mouth. "Yes, it is." He smiled. "Sometimes I surprise myself."

She looked away because she didn't want him to see

how pleased she was by his presence. "I'm perfectly capable of taking care of myself."

Sunlight backlit his hair. It was one of the few times she'd seen him without a cowboy hat.

"I have no doubt." He paused for a moment to chew. "But sometimes it's good to know someone cares."

She set her fork down, something about his words causing her to look down at her empty plate. He always managed to take her breath away with his kindness.

"I'll be back to cook you dinner, if that's okay. I can't promise much, but it's the effort that counts."

"You don't have to do that."

"I told you, I want to."

"I can cook, too."

"I'm sure you can." He smiled after taking another bite. "I'm sure you could hire a cook if you wanted to. You could arrange for a meal service. Go out and get fast food."

Did he know about her recent addiction? She hoped not. As often as she went, that would be embarrassing.

"The point is I'm here to do all that."

"Why?" she felt the need to ask.

He set his fork down, met her gaze. "You know, my aunt said something the other day. Said you surprised her. That you were a hard worker despite being born with a silver spoon in your mouth...or words to that effect."

She didn't know how to feel about his backhanded compliment. Flattered, she supposed. She had a feeling his aunt wasn't easily surprised by people.

"But it struck me that she was wrong."

She stared into his eyes, transfixed.

"You're not some spoiled little rich girl, are you?

Sure, your family loves you, and sure, you were born to wealth, but I have a feeling nothing's been handed to you over the years, sort of like me."

Her jaw almost dropped, because he was right, and it was something people never guessed, likely because they would never think the daughter of racing royalty would have to work for something. All they saw was her famous father and his big race team and her own career and presumed it'd all be handed to her. But her father and mother had never handed her anything.

"You've had to work hard to get where you are. I've only met your dad once, but he doesn't strike me as the type to let his kid drive for his team unless he or she was damn good at it. But you're a woman in a man's world and it's hard for people to believe you got there on your own merit, that you're just as good a driver as the men." He shook his head, his blue eyes turned light by the sun. "People never think that, do they?"

"No," she whispered. How had he seen her so clearly? Why did the fact that he did, despite all the trouble she'd given him, make her heart swell in a way that was impossible to ignore?

"But this is one instance where you don't have to do it all on your own." He leaned forward. "I'm not going to let you push me away anymore, Kait. I'm going to be here every morning, afternoon and night, job permitting. I'm going to take care of you and our babies and when you're given the all clear to leave, I'll drive you to North Carolina myself."

"No, Shane—"

"Shhh." He got up, went to her side of the table, and suddenly her heart began to pound. "Racing is a team sport. Raising a kid takes a team, too. So we're going to do it together. I'm not sure how, exactly, but I'm going to make sure that it all works out. You have my word on that."

She didn't know what to say. He always took that extra step for her. Marrying her when he didn't have to. Arranging for her to live on the ranch when he could have told her to find her own place. Protecting her. Caring for her. Loving her.

She stared down at her hands.

Well, not *love* love. The other kind of love, the kind that made her heart dance and her skin heat and her thighs tingle to the point that she had to press them together.

"Come on," he said. "I'll drive you up to the house. I'm sure my aunt is expecting you."

"Shane, wait."

She didn't know how much she'd missed touching him until she held out her hand and, God help her, he took it. She felt it again, that connection that was more like touching the live end of a wire. The buzz through her body and the warmth that followed.

"What?" he asked gently.

She swallowed. "I miss you."

There. She'd said it. As hard as the words had been to admit, she'd put it out there. It wasn't that she was lonely. She had all the company she wanted on the family ranch. No. It was that she ached for him. Wanted to be with him. Needed to touch him.

She felt him move. A hand cupped her cheek and this...*this* was what she wanted from him. The soft stroke of his fingers. The warmth of his body next to her own. The knowledge that he wanted her, not because she was Kait Cooper, famous race-car driver, but because he saw her. Her. It was as potent as an aphrodisiac.

"Kait," he said softly.

He drew her up and she let him. She was tired of fighting it. Tired of having to constantly be on guard. Tired of being Kait Cooper. She just wanted to be Kait. *His* Kait.

"I'm going to kiss you again, Kait," he said, staring into her eyes. "But I won't if you still want me to stay away."

It was strange because as she stared into his eyes she felt just as on edge, just as aroused, just as full of anticipation as the first night she'd met him.

"Make love to me, Shane."

Chapter Seventeen

His hands shook as he undressed her. She was the most beautiful woman in the world to him. Probably to a lot of guys, but she was his, and he marveled at the fact that he was the one tugging her T-shirt off. That she arched into him when he worked the button of her jeans. That she closed her eyes when his fingers touched her belly.

He couldn't resist bending down, inhaling the scent of her. Strawberries.

Don't kiss her. Not yet.

Because if he kissed her, he'd lose control and he didn't want that. Today he needed to show her that she wasn't alone, that she would *never* be alone.

And so he pulled the straps of her bra off her shoulders, touching her as gently as he could, slowly teasing a reaction out of her. He watched as she closed her eyes and tipped her head back, and for a moment he marveled that he held Kaitlin Cooper in his arms.

"You're so beautiful," he told her gently.

She started to shake her head, and he realized she didn't do so out of humility but because she genuinely didn't believe him.

"I've gotten fat."

He thought he misheard her at first.

But when she looked him in the eyes he knew he hadn't. Her body had changed and it had upset her, but if anything, she looked even more feminine these days. Curvy. Soft. Like a woman.

"You're perfect."

To prove his point, he bent down and kissed her belly, marveling that beneath his lips two little lives grew. Her skin was as soft as the petals of a flower. Her belly contracted at the touch of his lips. He moved them lower, kissing her again, smelling her and tasting her, his hands sliding up her bare legs, goose bumps sprouting beneath his touch. He stood, leaning her back and onto the bed. She sank down willingly.

Crazy.

He wanted to touch her all over, but with a gentleness that belied the urgency in his blood. So he told himself to slow down, moved up so he could kiss her, once, twice, as she tilted her head sideways and opened her mouth, and he marveled at how much she always tasted and smelled like strawberries. He palmed her breast, loving how full she was to the touch. His other hand cupped the back of her head, and he swore to the good Lord above, he could go on kissing her all day.

Her hand slipped between them, her fingers working on his buttons, and all the while they kept kissing and kissing, and somehow she got his shirt off and then his jeans and his boots until they were flesh to flesh.

He drew back then. She'd left her hair down and it lay around her head like a skein of silk. Her eyes were the blue of hydrangeas in the summer with a circle of lighter blue around her pupils. They were big, those eyes, and complemented by high cheekbones and the smallest of chins. She was, to him, perfect in every way.

He sank down to kiss her again, shifted his body, and she closed her eyes as their bodies fit together like the pieces of a puzzle. She arched into him and their hips grazed each other. Shane reached for her hands, to hold on to them because it felt like he might fall, and soon he was falling, though he'd told himself to take his time. But with her, there was no such thing as time. There was only her and the taste of her and feel of her and when he heard her cry out, he did, too.

"Shane," she sighed, arching into him.

Never, not ever, had it been like this with another woman. When he finally came back to earth he found himself staring into her eyes again.

"I wanted to take it slow," he said.

She smiled. "We never do anything slow."

He smiled, too. She had a point. So he shifted sideways, pulling her up against him, his chin in her hair.

"It's not fair," he heard her say. "All you have to do is touch me and I'm lost."

He knew how she felt. He'd tried to take it slowly, he really had, but it'd proven impossible.

"I think I should move to North Carolina."

Though she hadn't moved, he sensed her shock. It made him draw back to look into her eyes, and in them, he saw surprise and disbelief and maybe even a little fear.

"I know it's a big move, but I think we should try to make this work. For the babies' sake."

Liar, said a little voice in his head. The babies had nothing to do with this. It was all about *her*…and what they might have together. His aunt was right. Some things were worth taking a chance.

"But—" her eyes searched his own "—what about your life here?"

"The ranch will survive without me."

"So you would just give it up. Your family. Your job. The ranch."

"I won't be giving up my job. I'll still ride. There are rodeos on the East Coast. And I can find a job at a ranch anywhere."

"You would do that for me?"

He knew in that instant that he would do anything for her. "If you'll let me."

She smiled, a blinding grin unlike any he'd ever seen on her face before, her hand slipping up to cup his face. "Yes."

THE NEWS THAT Shane would be moving to North Carolina did not go over very well, or so Kait thought. That next week, as she worked on the cutting horse show with his aunt, she could tell Shane's father disapproved. Whenever the two of them were together, he didn't have a whole lot to say, not that he ever had a lot to say, but still…his disappointment was obvious.

"Don't let him get you down," Crystal said, a woman who reminded her so much of her mother she found herself opening up to her more and more. They were standing beneath a tent they'd erected in front of the main barn. Crystal had explained that they always kicked off their annual horse show with a wine-and-cheese meet and greet, so there were dozens of cowboys and cowgirls around them, each holding a glass of wine, some of them with a plate in hand, all of them laughing and smiling and clearly having a good time. She'd never felt like more of an outsider in her life. Horse people, she had decided, were all a little crazy about the animals they loved. Problem was, she didn't know a thing about them. Ergo, she had nothing in common with anyone other than Shane's family. Although she would have to admit, it was nice not to be the center of attention. Frankly, she wondered if anyone knew she drove race cars for a living. If they did, they didn't seem impressed.

"He'll learn to live with Shane's decision," Crystal added.

"I hope so." For Shane's sake. She could tell he'd taken his father's disapproval hard, but Shane's determination to make their situation work was yet one more thing to admire about him, and she had to admit, lately there was a lot.

He stood off to the side, talking to an older woman with long blond hair and boots that nearly reached her knees. He was laughing at something she had said, his own boots polished, his jeans pressed, the shirt he wore wrinkle-free. This was, she had learned, one of the premier cutting-horse events in the nation. Why that surprised her she had no idea, but she'd learned a lot about the Gillian Ranch and the various businesses over the past week or so. The family wasn't just wealthy, they were loaded, and yet Shane was so humble and genuinely nice. She'd met people with far less money, sponsors who thought they were all that and a bag of chips, who weren't half as down to earth.

"You're being summoned."

She'd been so deep in thought she hadn't noticed Shane motioning her over. She smiled a farewell to Crystal and moved to his side.

"No, really," he was saying to the woman. "She's actually really famous."

The woman had a wide smile, but her eyes were full of disbelief. "You drive race cars?"

"I do."

"In fact," Shane said. "There's a big race near LA next weekend. We're going to go watch her brother race."

"Wow. I'm impressed."

"Don't be," Kait said. "It's just a job."

It was something she said frequently, and yet it'd been nearly two months since she'd been grounded from racing, and she had more of an appreciation for what she did for a living than she'd ever had in her life. She missed it. Terribly. Next weekend would probably be hell. So close to what she loved and yet so far.

"Well, I'm impressed," the woman said.

"This is Sue Keller, by the way," Shane said. "She was last year's futurity winner."

"Really?" Kait smiled. "Now it's my turn to be impressed."

"Do you ride?"

"No."

"Kait hates horses," Shane said.

"I don't hate them."

"Okay, she's afraid of them."

The woman looked at her as if Shane had just told her she ate children for breakfast. "You're kidding."

"Nope."

She elbowed Shane. He laughed, and Kait turned and froze because as she watched him, eyes bright, chuckles escaping from deep in his chest, it hit her.

She loved him.

She very nearly took a step back.

No, she told herself. Impossible. It was just hormones. She couldn't love a man she'd known for…what? A few months.

"Maybe you should make him drive your race car," Sue said, clearly sympathizing with her embarrassment.

"I'd do that in a heartbeat," he quipped.

She had to force herself to focus. "Yes, well—" *focus* "—if he lets me ride a bull, I'll let him drive my race car."

Shane snorted. "I'll get back to you on that after the babies are born."

"You're pregnant?" Sue asked.

Kait nodded, her hands shaking as she patted her belly because she couldn't get the words out of her mind.

In love.

With the father of her children.

"I am."

"How far along?"

"Three months."

Six more months before her life would change forever. Six more months of trying to figure it all out. Six months of wondering if she and Shane would work.

"Well, congratulations," said Sue, smiling at someone who waved her over and leaving Kait and Shane alone.

"What's wrong?" he asked, and the way his eyes grew instantly concerned made her insides go soft.

"Nothing."

But she lied, because she knew as she stared into his eyes that nothing would ever be the same again.

Chapter Eighteen

Something was wrong. Shane tried to put his finger on it all weekend, but he could never really figure it out. Only at night did things change.

At night everything was exactly perfect. But one evening, two days before they were due to leave for the race on the outskirts of Los Angeles, she cried in his arms.

"What is it?" he asked, cradling her, instantly worried. "Did I hurt you?"

She shook her head.

"Then what is it?"

She wouldn't look at him. He had to touch her chin with his finger and tip her face toward his own. "Kait, what did I do?"

"Nothing," she mumbled, eyes filled with tears. "You didn't do anything."

"Then what is it?"

He saw something flash in her eyes, something that made his heart stop for a moment, but then it was gone. "I'm just worried about tomorrow's doctor's appointment."

He relaxed for a moment, even though a part of him wondered if that was really it. But he was always anxious before a doctor's appointment, too, now more than ever. If everything looked good this week, she would be cleared to go home. Her home. His soon-to-be new home.

"I'm sure it'll be okay."

He pulled her to him and she instantly relaxed in his arms. This was as it should be, how he always hoped it would be, despite what his dad said about losing his own identity and becoming her lackey. His dad didn't know what he was talking about.

They received the good news they'd both been expecting. The twins' growth rate was exactly where it should be and Kait's blood work all looked good. More important, since she'd tolerated a moderate increase in activity, they saw no reason why she couldn't resume a more normal life.

"We could fly home with my parents after this weekend's race."

Though there was still a hint of a shadow in her eyes, her smile was contagious, the bounce to her step unmistakable. He hadn't realized until that moment just how much she'd missed her home state. Still, her lingering fear had him on edge. Did she worry about their future together? Was that it?

"I'll have to tell my dad, but it should be okay."

Though he winced inwardly at how that conversation would pan out. In the weeks since their initial conversation about Shane moving to North Carolina, his dad's mood hadn't improved. If anything, he'd become more standoffish. Maybe a trip to North Carolina was just what he needed. Maybe it was what they both needed. It wasn't like he'd be stuck there all the time. He could come back home if he wanted. Help his dad transition to a life without him.

Smooth things over.

But if anything, his dad became even more surly as the day for their departure to the Fontana, California, racetrack approached.

THE MORNING THEY LEFT, his dad hardly spoke two words to him as Shane helped feed horses and organize the work chart. Carson would be filling in for him for now, at least until they could hire someone to replace him.

"I can't believe you're really going to do this," said his dad, coming up behind him as he finished writing. "Son, I have to ask. Are you sure this is the right move?"

No. He wasn't sure. If he admitted to his dad just how terrified he really was, he'd never hear the end of it. "I'm sure, Dad."

"So I can't talk you out of it."

Shane set the dry-erase marker down, the pungent smell of it filling the air. He braced himself as he turned to face his father.

"I'll be flying home with her family as soon as the race is over."

"So this is it then."

"Dad, I'll be back…"

His dad cocked his cowboy hat. "Will you?"

"Of course."

Silence came over the barn, something that didn't happen very often where animals were concerned, but it was as if all the horses in their stalls listened for what would come next. But the truth was, Shane was terrified. He had no idea what to expect in North Carolina. He'd never left home, though, not even for college. He'd traveled back and forth from the local university, all the while working on the ranch. Crazy that this would be the first time that he was gone, truly gone.

"I guess I'm barking up the wrong tree, then."

"It'll be okay, Dad. Trust me."

He wished he felt as convinced as he sounded.

"YOU'LL SEE," KAIT SAID, pulling her baseball hat down low on her forehead. "Nobody will recognize me."

Shane almost laughed. With her blond hair and unique features, he doubted that would be true. She had no idea how beautiful she was…even with thick sunglasses and her hair pulled through the hole of her hat.

"I doubt that," he said.

"Unlike you." She seemed about ready to laugh, and he was relieved that she didn't seem as tense as she had been in recent days. "Nobody will have a problem recognizing you." She flipped the brim of his black cowboy hat.

Shane clutched at it. "Hey."

"Let's go."

They'd been allowed to park in the infield, not far from the garage area where he could hear race cars revving. Out on the massive track, fast-moving blobs of color jockeyed for position, and the top part of the roof was visible because the angle of the track was so steep. It had dawned a typical Southern California day. Bright sunshine reflected off the grandstands across from them. A breeze brought to them the scent of exhaust mixed, oddly enough, with the scent of barbecue. It was practice day, a time when drivers and their crews worked on the cars to get them going as fast as possible.

Kait waved to the guard who stood at an opening in a chain-link fence.

"Kait," the older man said, seeming to be genuinely surprised to see her, and thus proving Shane's theory that Kait Cooper would have been recognizable in a paper sack. "Didn't expect to see you here."

She smiled. "Rumors of my retirement have been grossly exaggerated." She patted her belly. "I'll be back next season."

"Good to hear," said the man in blue, his gaze catching on Shane. He held up a hand, and it occurred to Shane that he didn't know he was with Kait.

"Can I see your pass?" he asked sternly.

"What'd you do with it, Shane?"

The guard straightened. "Is he with you?"

Kait nodded. "This is my husband."

The man's whole demeanor changed. "Well, why didn't you say so? Go on in, son."

But they'd only walked about ten steps when they heard, "Oh. My. GOSH. It's KAIT COOPER."

And that was how Shane found himself surrounded by a group of race fans, although where they'd come from he had no idea, and they all wanted autographs. She became surrounded by dozens of people. It happened so fast all Shane could do was step back and watch it unfold. Kait smiled at them all. No. Not just smiled, she glowed.

She'd missed it.

He didn't realize until that moment just how much. She smiled and laughed and seemed so totally in her element that it gave him pause. Had life on his family's ranch been so stifling?

"Okay, folks, gotta go." She lifted her hands as if in surrender. "My mom and dad don't even know I'm here yet."

There were groans, but he noticed she signed every single piece of paper thrust in her direction. She didn't just take off as if her fans were unimportant to her, something he'd seen many a famous cowboy do over the years.

He rushed to step up alongside of her because she took off so fast it was almost as if she'd forgotten he was with her. "So much for a disguise."

She shot him a wry grin. "No kidding, right? I thought since I'd been gone for so many weeks, people wouldn't think to look for me. Guess I was wrong."

In so many ways, Shane thought. As he followed her through the garage he saw many an eye trained her direction. Male. Female. They all seemed to know who she was. Those gazes frequently settled on him next, and Shane tried to ignore the feeling of being a bug under a microscope.

"Hey, Teddy," said Kait, stopping at the back of a big truck and trailer.

A man looked up, a handsome younger man, one with a smile that lit up his whole face. "Kait!"

And that was his first glimpse of Teddy Wright, Kait's crew chief, who was tan and buff in his red-and-white polo shirt and definitely *not* what he expected.

"Did you miss me?" she asked, sliding into his arms.

The two hugged, and Shane tried not to count off the seconds.

He's a coworker, he told himself. *They're probably longtime friends. Don't be jealous.*

Her mom came over next and then her dad, the whole family having been inside the big-rig trailer. Shane had never felt more like a third wheel than at that moment, watching as she was greeted by her teammates and her family and her friends.

"And this is Shane—"

He almost missed the introduction he'd been so deep in thought about why he felt so, so…put out.

"—my husband."

They didn't make him feel unwelcome. Far from it. Everyone smiled as he stepped forward and shook hands. They dragged Kait off shortly after, something about test data and needing her help, and he found himself standing at the back of a glorified car trailer trying to blend in while Kait disappeared inside the big rig.

"It'll get easier."

He half turned. Kait's mom stood over an ice chest near the back bumper of the big rig. She cracked the cap of an ice water.

"Want one?"

"No, thanks."

She closed the lid before taking a seat next to him.

"Trust me," she said, taking a sip. "I know what it's like to feel like a fish out of water."

She didn't look like one in her red shirt with a white star on her front. She looked like part of the team. Her red hair had been pulled off her head, her gray streaks more pronounced, and it was funny because he'd seen her at his ranch home, but for some reason she seemed different at the racetrack. More businesslike. Less like the mom he remembered.

"I have a feeling it'll take some getting used to."

"And don't worry about him." She pointed to her husband, who stood across a strip of asphalt talking to someone. Jarrod Cooper, he realized, his face as recognizable as his sister's. "He'll warm up to you."

Shane wasn't so certain. It would probably be a long time before Kait's dad forgave him for knocking up his little girl.

"I'm not sure that I blame him after everything that's happened."

Her mom tipped her head sideways, and it always amazed him how much she looked like Kait—but with red hair. "Yes, but now you're doing the right thing. You're here. You'll be going to North Carolina with her. Things will work out."

He was about to tell Kait's mom he felt the same way when he heard a man say, "You Shane Gillian?"

When he turned around he had a camera in his face. A television commentator stood next to the cameraman, some kind of earphone/antenna on his head, a microphone in one hand, what looked like a cell phone in the other.

"I'm Rex Tillman from RNTV. Racing Network," he clarified. "And I understand you're Kait's new husband? Care to share a few words?"

He honestly didn't know what to say. "About what?"

The man flicked a button on his mic, swiped something on his cell phone and then held it up. "Kait tells us you're going to work for Cooper Racing. That must be a big transition after riding bulls."

Whaaaa?

Kait's mom hopped out of her chair. "Now, Rex. None of that's decided yet." She sounded so sweet as she stepped in front of the camera. "Kait's husband just got here. Give him a second to assimilate the news."

News? What news?

"I'll do that if you talk to me about Jarrod's chances in the race," Rex said.

"Done," Sarah said with a smile at Shane. "Be right back."

Go to work for Cooper Racing? Give up bull riding? *What?*

Kait came out of the trailer then, her smile still in place. He crossed his arms over his chest.

"We need to talk."

Chapter Nineteen

"I just thought it might be easier than having to find a job all on your own in North Carolina," Kait said, trying not to wince at the anger on Shane's face. She'd never seen him mad before, although if she were honest with herself, she didn't really blame him. She hadn't meant to overstep her bounds, she'd just been trying to make his life easier. That was what you did when you cared for someone.

When you loved them.

She just hadn't told him yet.

"I didn't mean to upset you."

They were in the lounge of her brother's hauler, a flat-screen TV showing a pack of race cars out on the track, the sound a few seconds behind the actual noise out on the racetrack. With any luck, they'd be left alone, at least for a little bit. You never knew what team member might need to get into the tiny room that doubled as a storage area for team uniforms and other racing paraphernalia.

"I can find my own job working with cattle, just like before. You don't need to make one up for me. And, by the way, I'm riding this Saturday night. I'll be riding the following weekend somewhere in the South, too. I don't know where exactly, but I'll be entering some-where. *That's* my job."

"Yeah. About Saturday night." She forced a smile. "I don't think I can go. My dad set up a publicity appear-ance for the whole family. He asked me to attend. It's at some swanky hotel in Los Angeles. Long commute there. Another long drive back to the track afterward. I was thinking I could head out with my family while you go to your rodeo."

Another expression landed on his face—disappoint-ment. Maybe even dismay.

"That's too bad," was all he said, and in some ways that made it worse, because she knew he'd been looking forward to her watching him ride again. They'd talked about it on the way to the racetrack.

"I'm sorry, Shane." She took a deep breath, and be-cause she couldn't deny her feelings for him anymore, reached out and touched his hand. "I would have felt bad telling my dad no, especially after I've been gone for so long."

"No. That's all right." He still wore his cowboy hat and he used it to shield his eyes. "I understand."

She should get him a polo shirt and team baseball cap. Maybe that would make him feel better.

Don't be ridiculous, Kait. You've let him down. A shirt and ball cap won't help.

"Will it be televised?" she asked.

"No. It's just a local rodeo, Kait. Not a big race."

And something about his tone set her back up. "What's that supposed to mean?"

He shook his head. "Nothing." And then the fight seemed to drain out of him. His shoulders slumped and he stared down at the ground for a moment as if gathering his thoughts. "Look. I get it. You're famous. I'm just some cowboy from nowheresville, California. You have way bigger obligations than I have."

"That's not true. People know who you are."

"Not like they know who you are, Kait." He met her gaze again and his eyes were intense. "We couldn't even get ten feet inside the track before people were clamoring for your autograph."

"People ask for your autograph, too."

"Not unless we're at a rodeo. I can't take you anywhere without someone recognizing you. The store. The hospital. My own rodeos." He lifted a hand. "But that's not the point. My point is you have bigger obligations than I do. But when it comes to a job, Kait, one outside of rodeo, I can handle that on my own just as well as you can handle yours."

She stared down at the linoleum floor for a moment. Okay. So she might have overstepped her bounds by asking her dad to find Shane a job. She should have cleared it with Shane first.

"I'm sorry," she said again.

He came forward and his hands gently clasped her forearm. "It's okay." He bent down and she knew he was going to kiss her—

"Kait, your dad's looking for you."

They both jumped apart.

"He said he needs you to talk to Nate. Give him some pointers before he heads back out again."

Kait smiled up at him apologetically. She'd wanted him to kiss her. Everything seemed all right with the world when he touched her like he did.

"Duty calls," she said.

"It sure does."

When she slipped from his grasp, he let her go. She hated leaving him, though. Hated the look of regret and disappointment in his eyes, but this was her life. Always pulled in ten different directions. Running here and there. Some days she was lucky to have five minutes to herself.

He would have to get used to it. He had no other choice. She might love him, and he might love her, too… one day, but they would have to get used to what life would be like together. Otherwise…

She didn't want to think about otherwise.

HE HARDLY SAW HER. The only time they had to themselves was at night, and that first evening, she was so exhausted she practically fell asleep in his arms. He worried that she might be doing too much, but she reassured him the next morning that everyone kept an eye on her. When they arrived at the track, off she went again. He was left at the car trailer, which she called a "hauler," while she did another televised interview or a media appearance or attended a team meeting.

By Friday he felt so completely useless that when Carson called and asked if he'd be his roping partner, Shane jumped at the chance. Anything was better than just sitting around. Besides, it was at the same rodeo he was scheduled to compete at, so this way he'd get there early. No worries about travel time tomorrow.

"But…you'll miss qualifying in the afternoon," Kait said. He'd had to text her to find out where she was at, and he considered it a minor miracle that she'd managed to escape. He'd seen her for maybe ten minutes all day. Sarah Cooper said he'd get used to being on his own at the racetrack, and if he wasn't careful, they'd put him to work.

"I'm sure I can watch it on TV."

It was an echo of her own words to him the other day. He could tell she knew it, too.

"I wanted you to see it live."

"I know, and I'm sorry. But this works better for me. I won't have to drive to the rodeo tomorrow. I can just stay with my brother tonight."

He could tell she didn't like the idea, though. He'd never seen Kait pout before, but he was pretty sure that's what she was doing now.

"You promise you'll be back for the race on Sunday?" she asked.

"Scout's honor."

She nodded and looked like she might say something more, but then she must have changed her mind. Instead she reached up and kissed him on the cheek.

"See you Sunday, then."

WHEN HE PULLED into the rodeo grounds three hours later, Shane had to admit it was a relief. He hadn't realized until that exact moment just how out of place he'd felt in Kait's world.

Better get used to it, bud.

"You escaped," Carson said as he walked up to the truck and trailer. Hotrod turned his head when he spotted him. He held out a hand.

"Miss me, buddy?" he asked softly.

"Of course I did, Shane," said his brother. "I can't live without you."

He patted his horse on the neck. "I wasn't talking to you."

"I know." His brother shot him a smile.

"Who's up in the perf tonight?"

His brother shrugged, set his hat on his head a little more firmly. "Oh, the usual suspects. Miller and Hillard, and the Thomasin brothers. Ray and that new guy. Dustin, I think his name is."

Shane nodded. Three days off and he'd missed riding like hell. He didn't know how he'd deal in North Carolina. Hotrod and his truck and trailer would stay in California until he could find a place for his horse. He'd thought about not bringing Hotrod, but he needed a taste of home. He had a feeling having his horse around would help to keep him sane. Plus he might need his horse for his new job...wherever that might be.

"Everything going okay at the ranch?"

His brother nodded. "You know how it is with Dad, though. Never wants to admit how much he depends on you. Still won't admit how sorry he is that you left, not even with his health the way it is."

Shane had been about to head to the tack area to grab his saddle, but he stopped. It was late afternoon and the railing the horses were tied to was in shadow, but he could see into his brother's eyes perfectly.

"What do you mean?"

Carson drew back a bit, clearly surprised by the question.

"That heart thing he had this week."

It felt like he'd been zapped by a hot wire. "What heart thing?"

Any chance Carson was pulling his leg went completely out the window when he spotted the look on his brother's face. He was completely and utterly serious.

"How could you not know?" Carson asked.

"What is wrong with Dad's heart?" Shane asked, holding on to his patience by the thinnest of threads.

Carson shook his head a bit. "A few days ago, I think the same day you left with Kait, he started having chest pains. I thought everyone knew. He went in for some tests. Said it wasn't a heart attack, but he has some serious blockage going on. They're doing more tests on Monday."

He hadn't been told. Hadn't even been called. Not even by his aunt.

"You didn't know?"

"No clue."

His brother seemed taken aback. "Wow. He must be more mad at you than I thought."

Shane winced because if Carson-Who-Didn't-Have-a-Care-in-the-World had noticed his dad giving him the cold shoulder, everyone else probably knew, too. That was probably why nobody had called. He would bet everyone had been told not to tell him.

"Why didn't you call me?"

Carson shrugged. "I just assumed you'd know." He stroked his chin. "Although come to think of it, I did wonder why you hadn't checked on him this week."

There were days when he really wanted to hit his brother. This was one of them.

"Look, I wouldn't worry about it. We've got it covered. I mean, you might want to phone the old man and let him know you're thinking of him, but I'll keep you posted on what the doctors tell him."

The news took the wind out of his sails. Heart problems. And he hadn't told him.

It was hard to focus on roping after that. His brother, usually not very perceptive, must have sensed his troubled mood, because he didn't say a word when Shane missed his steer. No paycheck for the Gillian brothers that weekend.

"Are you sure it's his heart?" Shane asked because, honestly, the thought went through his head that his dad could be faking it just to make him feel bad about leaving. Anything was possible with his dad.

But then why didn't he tell me?

"No. They're sure. They think he had a blockage of some sort."

Shane jumped off his horse. "And his tests are on Monday."

Carson did the same, but he paused in the middle of loosening his horse's girth. "Wait. You're not thinking of sticking around, are you?"

Of course he was. He and his dad might not see eye to eye on some things, but that didn't mean he didn't care. And if his dad was down for the count, that meant extra work at the ranch, and they were already down one man.

"Maybe."

"Don't do that." Carson turned to face him fully. "We've got this. If it's anything serious, I'll give you a call and you can fly home."

But he was already shaking his head. "No." He couldn't do it. He couldn't take off when his dad might be in trouble.

KAIT FELT THE same way when he talked to her later.

"Stay," she said, her voice low and sexy, although in reality she was probably just exhausted. "I'm sorry you'll miss your first race, but you're doing the right thing. Stay."

Was that relief he felt?

"I'll call you when I know a little more."

She didn't say anything.

"Kait?" he asked, wondering if they'd lost their connection.

"I'm here. I just wanted to tell you…" She paused again. "I just want to say that I…"

His heart pounded.

"…I hope your dad is okay. And I'm sorry you got bucked off your bull."

He let out a breath. "Thanks. And you have a safe trip back home."

He stared at his cell phone long after they'd hung up. What had she been about to say? For some reason he didn't think it was to wish his dad well.

Shane, I…

Love you.

That was what it sounded like she'd been about to say. And if she did, what then? It was good news given what they had planned for the future.

Only for some reason, it didn't feel good. It felt terrifying.

Chapter Twenty

"So is he staying another week in California?" her mom asked two weeks later.

Kait hung up the phone and turned, trying to hide her disappointment. "Yeah." She sighed. "Just until his dad is back on his feet again. I guess the surgery hit him harder than expected."

Her mother nodded in understanding, but as Kait swiveled her chair to face the glass window that overlooked Cooper Racing's main shop, she wondered…

"It's not easy when it finally happens, is it?"

She turned to face her mom again, and for a moment she contemplated playing dumb. She knew what her mom was saying. It didn't make it any easier to admit, but she knew. She and her mom never kept secrets from each other.

"I thought it would be different," Kait admitted. "I thought falling in love meant happily-ever-after."

Her mom sat in a chair opposite Kait's desk. Kait had had her own office at Cooper Racing since the day she'd signed on as a driver. It was covered in mementos from her racing career; from her first peewee go-kart trophy to her most recent win in Michigan. Photos were on her desk. In the winner's circle. At a family wedding. Out with her family on vacation on the Colorado ski slopes.

"Trust me, Kait. No relationship is perfect."

"You and Dad seem pretty happy."

Her mom huffed with laughter. "Because you don't live with us any longer. Believe me, it's no fairy tale. We had our share of struggles, mostly after you kids were born and I was the one having to stay home all the time. It was tough on me. Your father is a very good-looking man. I always worried some other woman might turn his head."

"So what'd you do?"

She shrugged. "I had to learn to trust him. And after a while, it got easier, but there was always that fear."

"You don't have to worry about that, Mom. Dad loves you."

"And Shane loves you, too."

Kait felt her jaw go slack. "What makes you say that?"

"Just a hunch." Her mom nodded. "I think he felt completely overwhelmed at the race in California."

Kait picked up a snow globe she'd gotten overseas. The Tower Bridge became barely visible thanks to a sudden snowstorm.

"He'd have to learn to get used to it," she said, shaking the globe and watching the tiny white specks dance around. She felt a lot like she lived in a snow globe right now. Completely off-kilter. Shaken up. Unable to see things clearly.

"You couldn't have picked a guy more different than you," her mom observed. "Never been to a race in his life. Rides bulls. Lives in California."

All things she'd been thinking herself. "I didn't mean for it to happen."

Her mom leaned back in her chair. "So? What are you going to do?"

Kait shrugged. "Wait and see, I guess."

Her mom snorted. "Since when have you ever waited to see if something would work out?"

Kait just shook her head. "What choice do I have?"

"You could go see him."

"And say what? I love you? Don't leave me? Come join me and my crazy life?"

"That would be a start."

Kait got up from the chair, and as always happened, her hand landed on her belly. Her doctor said not to freak out that she seemed bigger than a house already. She was carrying twins. She needed to cut herself some slack, but it was strange to feel the way her belly protruded and to wear clothes with elastic in the waist and to be so off balance. She hated it.

"If he wanted to be here, he'd be here."

"So you're just going to let him go?"

She didn't know, damn it, so she shrugged. There was a reason she hadn't told Shane she loved him. She didn't want to be the one to chase him around. Or make him feel obligated to say it back. She was romantic enough to want him to want *her*.

"What if he doesn't love me?" she asked.

It was her biggest fear. That he'd tell her he didn't want a relationship with her. That he'd be a dad to their babies, but that would be it.

"There's no way any man in his right mind wouldn't want you." Her mom shook her head. "But the circus that goes along with you?" Her mom frowned. "That's a different matter entirely."

And that was it in a nutshell. That was the fear that kept her up at night. He'd gotten a taste of her life in California, and she hadn't even been driving a race car. If anything, her life was more chaotic then.

"I don't want to lose him, Mom."

"Then go after him, honey."

"Why am I terrified about doing that?"

"Because you love him. It's hard to let it all hang out there, Kait. Probably one of the hardest things you'll ever have to do, but you need to tell him. And you need to let him say it back…or not."

Her mom was right. She needed to go to California and lay it all out. She just wished that snow globe doubled as a crystal ball because if Shane didn't love her, well, she didn't know what she'd do.

"HE LOOKS GOOD," Reese Gillian said, leaning against the rail of their arena, despite the doctor's orders to take it easy. He'd been lucky. The procedure he'd undergone had been one of the less invasive ones. His dad told people he'd had his pipes cleaned out. Still, he was supposed to be off his feet for a few more days. Shane's dad didn't know the meaning of the words *bed rest*.

"I think he's going to be a good one." Shane reached down and straightened a piece of the sorrel's long mane. "He's definitely futurity material. I think he'll be ready to compete this fall."

"If you keep riding him."

He didn't want to have this conversation with his dad. Not again. He'd agreed to stay on to help out until his dad was back on his feet. The doctor had said Reese needed three to four weeks before he could resume exercising. That meant at least another month of being away from Kait.

You could visit her.

But the thought of flying out to North Carolina, and of jumping back into Kait's life... He didn't know if he could do it. Didn't know if he was man enough to always take a backseat to his famous wife. The realization had made him want to vomit, but he could no longer deny it. The longer he stayed away, the more he recognized his own fears. He was terrified of falling in love with his own wife.

"You'll find someone else who's just as good with the colts as I am, Dad. I can't promise anything."

Couldn't he, though? Hadn't he decided it was better to distance himself from Kait? Now? Before he got in too deep? He still planned to take care of her. To help raise their kids. He'd never shirk from that responsibility, but more than that? He honestly didn't know.

"Who's that?"Reese asked.

Shane followed the direction of his dad's gaze.

And froze.

There could be no doubt who walked toward him. Her long hair was unmistakable. In the afternoon sunlight, it lit up like autumn leaves. Her body, though, that had changed. He couldn't believe how much. And on the heels of that thought came a flood of guilt that he hadn't been there to watch it happen.

"Is that Kait?" his dad asked.

"It is."

His dad glanced back at him, but there was no disappointment in the eyes beneath the cowboy hat. Or recrimination. Or dismay. There was just fear.

His dad was terrified.

It was like suddenly being hit by a wrecking ball. His whole body reacted to the realization that his dad didn't want him to stick around because he worried about Shane's rodeo career. He was afraid of losing him to another family.

She was so close now that he could see into Kait's eyes. Shane slipped off his horse.

"Give us a moment, Dad."

He would analyze what he'd gleaned later, after he talked to Kait, because if she was here in California, this wasn't a social call. She'd come a long way to talk to him. It must be serious.

His dad tipped his hat at Kait as he walked by. Shane didn't move. He stood there, holding the reins of the colt he'd been training. His heart beating in tune with her steps.

"Shane."

That was all she said, coming to a stop a few feet away. No smile. No real greeting. No pithy comment about the weather.

He'd been avoiding her. Sure, his dad had been sick, but that first week he could have slipped away to see her. For sure he could have done so the second week. It wasn't like he was hurting for money. He'd won more than his fair share of purses this spring.

"How you been?"

She patted her belly. "We've been fine."

No doubt about it, she wasn't happy with him, and he didn't blame her. Sure, he'd called. They'd spoken on the phone. So he hadn't completely abandoned her. And it wasn't like he didn't have a good excuse for going MIA. Still.

"I'm surprised to see you here."

She tipped her head sideways, and he knew she would dive right into what was on her mind. That was the way she did things.

"What happened, Shane? One minute you're all set to move to North Carolina and the next I hardly hear from you."

He winced. "My dad was sick."

"I know your dad's been sick. Your aunt's been keeping me in the loop. She said he's doing okay now, and he looked pretty good to me. A little paler than usual, but okay. So you could have left for North Carolina this week if you'd wanted to."

He was tempted to deny it, but he prided himself on being honest. It was time to put it all out there.

"Kait, look." He fiddled with the edge of the reins. "I just don't think I can do it."

She tilted her chin up. It was the same pose he'd seen in magazines and on billboards. Kait Cooper: big bad race-car driver.

"So you're staying here?"

"For now." He shrugged, but it was hard not to feel bad about the situation. He'd told her he'd be there for her, and he'd planned to do exactly that, but then he'd gone to the race, and for some reason things had changed.

"When the babies come, I'll be there. No doubt. And afterward, we can work out a schedule. And if you need me before then, you know you only have to call."

Some of the bravado faded. Another expression entered her eyes. It gave him pause, made him brace for her next words.

"But I love you, Shane."

It was then at that moment that he understood what he'd seen in her eyes. Heartbreak.

"Kait, I—"

"No." She held up a hand. "Hear me out. I love you. I've known it for awhile now, I was just too stubborn to say it." She inhaled deeply, and he realized she was fighting to hold herself together. "I had some stupid idea that the man should be the first one to say it. But now I'm wondering, if I'd said it earlier, maybe you might be saying something different to me now. If it might *still* get you to say something different."

She was Kait Cooper. Famous race-car driver. A woman who could have any man in the world, and she was baring her soul to him because she loved him. He could barely breathe for a moment.

"Kait, please—"

"No," she said. "Don't say another word. I can see how you feel about me in your eyes."

And it wasn't that he didn't love her back. But when it came right down to it, he knew their lives were too different. He was just saving them both future heartbreak. Wasn't he?

"I just think it's better if we keep to our original deal. I'll be there for you. And for our kids. Always."

Just not for you.

That was what her eyes accused him of, and he couldn't look at her. Call him a coward. Call him a jerk. Call him an idiot. This was Kait Cooper in front of him. Any other man would give his right leg to be with her. But he just couldn't say the words, the words she wanted to hear.

"So I guess I'll see you at the birth, then?"

There was a tinge of anger to her words. He didn't

blame her. He'd let her think they were headed in a different direction only to pull back at the last moment.

"I'll be there for the birth and for all your doctor's appointments. Text me the dates."

She stared up at him, her chin quivering. She held on to her tears by the barest of threads, he could see that, and it made him sick all over again. He'd hurt her.

"Kait…" He took a step toward her.

She pulled back. "I'll see you later, then, Shane." Her voice sounded strange. "Thanks for marrying me."

I wish you could have loved me, too.

He could see the words in her eyes, and for the first time, he felt close to tears, too.

"Kait…"

She turned and walked away.

Chapter Twenty-One

She cried the whole way home. Their pilot, Chuck, looked bewildered when they landed hours later. He'd probably spotted her tear-swollen eyes and red nose.

"Are you okay?"

"Fine," she lied.

Shane didn't love her.

She'd had no idea how hard that would hit her until the moment he'd stared down at her and told her how he'd be there for her.

The jerk.

That was the problem. She vacillated between anger and outrage and bitter, awful sadness. But the anger wasn't just about Shane. She was mad at herself, too. She'd been the one to go chasing after him. To confront him in California. She should have just kept her emotions to herself.

Chuck must have tipped off her mom, because Kait spotted her mom's familiar red Mustang out in front of her home. She almost turned around. She didn't need to cry anymore, but she knew she'd take one look at her mother's face and she'd break down again.

She was right.

Stupid, stupid, stupid.

That was what she kept calling herself as she stood out in her driveway, protected by her mom's loving arms. How could she have blundered things so badly? Pregnant. Married. Unlovable.

"Shush," her mom said. "You are not unlovable."

She hadn't even realized she'd spoken the words out loud. Her mom had drawn back, a look of admonishment on her face. They sun had begun to set, the surface of the water off the back of her house a brilliant, iridescent gold.

"I just don't understand what I did wrong."

"You did nothing wrong." Her mom shook her shoulders a bit. "Well, aside from getting pregnant and marrying a perfect stranger and then moving in with that man before you had a chance to know who he was."

She wouldn't have thought it was possible, but she actually smiled at her mom's words. "Oh, is that all?" She wiped at her tears with the palm of her hand.

Her mom smiled, too. "Honey, the odds were against you from the start." The smile turned tender. She swiped a lock of Kait's hair back, just like she'd been doing since she was a little girl. "You more than anyone should know what it's like to start out as an underdog. It's not your fault things didn't work out. It just wasn't meant to be."

But it'd felt like it should have been meant to be. Looking back on it, she wondered if she'd fallen in love with Shane at first sight. She'd never done what she'd done with him with another man. Never taken one look at a man's dark, handsome looks and fallen...hard.

"I'm going to be a single mom."

"No." Sarah tipped her nose down so they were inches apart. "You have us. You have your racing family, too. You'll even have Shane. The man doesn't strike me as they type to shirk his responsibilities. He'll be there for you and the kids."

He would be. She knew that, and her eyes filled with tears again. "But seeing him, Mom. Knowing he doesn't want to be with me that way. I don't know if I'll be able to bear it."

"You'll bear it just fine." Kait found herself pulled forward again, into her mom's arms. "You're one of the strongest women I know, Kait. I've watched you do things over the years that have left me in awe. I sometimes wonder, where does she get it from? How did your dad and I make someone so amazing and wonderful and unique? I have no doubt you'll be just as amazing a mother as you are a person and a race-car driver. Single or no. With Shane or without. You'll do fine. I have no doubt at all."

The words had her wiping away tears. If her mom thought she was amazing, that was nothing compared to how Kait felt about Sarah Cooper.

"I hope I'll raise my kids just like you did."

The hug grew tighter. "You will."

Just without Shane. Without a husband. It broke her heart.

TRUE TO HIS WORD, he was there for her next doctor's appointment. He'd said he'd meet them there, and he did, but there'd been a part of Kait that wished he had reneged on his offer.

"It's okay," said her mom, reaching for her hand as they watched Shane approach, all dark and dangerous cowboy in his black hat and black jeans and black sideburns. Every female eye in the doctor's office followed his progress. Kait just felt sick.

"Hey there," he said, coming up to her side. "Mrs. Cooper." He smiled and nodded at her mom.

"Shane," her mom said, a wheelbarrow full of disappointment and sadness and anger in that one word.

Shane heard it. His polite smile faltered.

"How's your dad?" Kait asked as he took a seat next to her.

"Fine, fine." He picked up a magazine. She felt his presence next to her like she would a bear at an exhibit at a zoo.

She was never more grateful than when a nurse called, "Mrs. Gillian?" The last thing Kait wanted was to sign autographs this morning.

"You want me to go with you?" asked her mom.

"No, that's okay." They hadn't been sure Shane would show up, but now that he was here…

"Right this way," the nurse said. Kait could tell the woman tried to ignore Shane's presence, but she kept sneaking glances at him.

"You look sort of familiar," she said, but she wasn't looking at Kait with her big blue eyes. Oh, no. When she opened the door of a room, she stared at Shane, who shook his head.

"Really?" he said. "Don't think we've met."

"You're from California," the nurse said, pointing at Kait to take a seat on the paper-covered exam table. "I recognize your accent."

"You're the one with an accent," he joked. "And I am from California. Via Del Caballo, actually."

The woman seemed puzzled. Okay, Kait would admit it. She was beautiful with her dyed black hair and fake eyelashes. They had to be fake. They were just too thick to be natural.

"Do you work for a race team?"

If she weren't so heartbroken Kait would have laughed. Shane couldn't seem to take his eyes off the nurse. It stung. There was no comforting hand on her shoulder. No silent stare of reassurance. It was as if she didn't exist. She had to clench her hands to keep the emotion from her eyes.

"Nope."

The nurse had gone to a cabinet. She handed Kait a paper robe. "Change into this," she said without glancing at her. She still stared at Shane. "I'll be back in a second to take your pulse and blood pressure."

She left with one last long stare, and Kait could only shake her head. The woman had to know Shane was the father of her babies. Or maybe not, because she noticed then that Shane didn't wear his wedding ring.

She gulped, took a deep breath.

Okay, enough, she told herself. *He's here. He's doing his duty. That's all that matters.*

"I'll just turn my back," he said.

"Thanks," she answered, but the word sounded choked out even to her own ears.

She felt self-conscious, though, as she changed. Stupid thing to feel, given the circumstances.

Someone knocked. She heard the nurse say, "You ready?" but she didn't even wait for an answer, just opened the door.

"All right, then." She scanned the chart, but only after she looked at Shane again. "You're five months along. Ooo. How exciting." For the first time, their eyes met. "You'll find out the sex of your babies today."

She looked down at Kait's chart again. But then the woman straightened, her eyes having caught on a piece of paper in there, and Kait thought for sure she'd finally recognized her.

"You're Shane Gillian," the woman said. "That's why you look so familiar." She very nearly pointed. "I watched you at the NFR last year. I mean, like. I was there. In Las Vegas."

From nowhere came the urge to laugh. Here she was, one of Charlotte, North Carolina's, most famous faces, and *who* had been recognized?

"I'm a huge fan of bull riding, Mr. Gillian. Wait." She turned toward Kait. "If he's Shane that means that you're…"

The woman stared between the two of them. "Wow. I read about you two in *Celebrity Now!*"

Celebrity Now? They'd been featured in that trashy rag?

"Some power sports couple thing. But wow. Here you are in front of me. I can't believe it."

It was as if someone had pulled the plug on Kait's temper. She wanted to laugh. It was all so surreal. Shane being here with her. A nurse who was a big fan of his. The whole crazy situation of being married to him, but not really.

The nurse, whose name was Marion, wrapped the blood-pressure cuff around her arm, chattering the whole time. Occasionally Kait would be forced to respond, but Marion directed most of her comments at Shane.

"Everything looks good," Marion said with a smile that reached her blue eyes. "The ultrasound technician will be here in a second, so I have to ask. Do you want to know the sex of your babies?"

Was that how Shane had felt back in California? Kait wondered. When fans had surrounded her and wanted her attention? Did he feel the same spurt of jealousy that she had just felt?

"Kait?" Shane asked.

"Yes," she heard herself say. "I'd like to know."

Shane nodded, a slight smile playing with his lips. "I'd like to know, too."

"Terrific." The nurse wrote something down in her chart. "Tara will be here in just a second."

And they were alone.

"If you'd rather not find out…" Shane said.

"No, no." She took a deep breath. For some reason she felt like she'd been given a clue to an important piece of a puzzle, but damned if she knew what it was. "I want to know."

They didn't have any more time to discuss it because an older woman came in with a wide smile on her face. "I hear you want to know the gender of your babies." Her smile included both of them as she urged Kait to lie back. "How exciting."

It hit her then. She would always have her babies. Shane might leave her, she might be on her own, but she would always have the two precious lives.

"Okay, here we go."

The liquid she spread on Kait's belly was warm, the paper robe she wore crinkling as Tara's hand moved around. Kait's heart had started to pound for a whole other reason, her sadness fading into anticipation when Tara grabbed a plastic wand.

"Twins, right?" Tara asked.

"Yes," Shane answered, and he sounded as tense as she felt.

"Okay. Just so you know, sometimes one twin will block the other which can make it difficult to…" The nurse smiled. "Nope. There's a good view of one of them right now. And look at that," she smiled at them both. "A little boy."

Kait wanted to cry. She wanted to reach for Shane's hand. He must have read her mind, though, because his fingers clutched her own and it felt so good and so right and so wonderful to be held by him, even if it didn't really mean anything. She clutched his hand back.

"Okay, let me see if I can get a good view of the… Well, there it is. There's the other one." Tara's smile grew delighted. "A little girl. Fraternal twins. How exciting."

She was crying. She didn't know why. When she looked up at Shane, she saw that he was, too.

"Congratulations." The nurse moved the wand around some more. "And they look great, too. Heart looks great. Bones are all normal. All good signs."

"Thank you," Shane said.

"My pleasure. I'll have your images up front when you check out. The doctor will need to look them over, too. He'll be in shortly."

And they were alone.

"A boy and a girl," Kait said. "My mom's going to be so excited. She'll be able to buy things in both sections of the baby store."

Shane let go of her hand. It was if the temperature in the room had dropped twenty degrees.

"It's good they're healthy."

"Yes, it is."

He broke her heart all over again. For some reason, sharing that brief moment of intimacy, looking into his eyes and seeing joy, and now…nothing.

"My aunt and sister were wondering if they could throw you a baby shower in California."

She took a deep breath. Enough. No more moping.

"Actually, my mom and a few of the wives are throwing me one here. But I'll be sure to send them an invitation, though. They can fly out if they want."

Shane nodded. "I'll tell them."

The doctor came in next, and he went over her chart and what to expect in the coming weeks, and when it was all said and done, they stood in the room alone. Two people responsible for the two tiny lives growing inside her belly…and yet with nothing to say to each other.

"So I'll see you next month?" he asked.

"Sure." She nodded. "And I'll be sure to send your aunt and sister an invite."

He nodded. She waited.

"Let me know if you need anything."

"I will."

He leaned toward her and her heart stopped, but the kiss he placed on her cheek was quick and impersonal. She closed her eyes all the same.

"See you next month."

He was gone when she opened her eyes, and Kait stared at the spot where he'd been and told herself not to cry. The next visit would be easier. Things would go smoother from here on out. She would get used to seeing him while her heart was breaking inside.

She *had* to.

Chapter Twenty-Two

What a chump.

That was what he thought the whole way home. It didn't matter how many times he told himself things were better this way. That they were just two different people with two very different lives and that it would never work out, not in the long run, at least. He'd done the right thing calling the whole thing off.

Yet he couldn't get her heartbroken, shattered, disappointed eyes out of his mind.

When he arrived in California he almost picked up the phone to call her. Twice. But what purpose would it serve? He'd made his decision. So, as he drove back to the ranch, he kept reciting to himself that he'd done the right thing. His dad would be proud. He'd behaved responsibly.

But for the rest of the week and then into that weekend, it took every ounce of his willpower not to call her. When he won his rodeo that weekend, he wanted to call her. When Carson missed roping the heels of his steer, he wanted to call her. When he got home late that night and the stars were so bright he could have sworn he could pluck them from the sky, he wanted to call her.

What the hell was wrong with him?

That next morning, he dreaded the family barbecue. So much so that when he arrived later that afternoon, he hid out on the side of the house. There was a huge oak tree there, one with a picnic bench beneath it. He had a great view of the valley below—of the stables and the vineyard and the arena. And he was all alone.

Or so he thought.

"You went to see her."

He nearly groaned. Just what he needed. His dad.

"And you came back," his dad added.

Shane glanced at the table where he sat. It was only then that he realized what he'd been carving in the surface.

S + K.

His dad saw it, too, as he sat down opposite him, and Shane realized his dad had aged in the previous weeks. Heart surgery had finally allowed Father Time to catch up to him. His gray hair seemed to have gotten more gray. The wrinkles on his face were more pronounced. His skin had yet to regain a healthy glow.

"I'm having a son and a daughter, Dad."

His dad looked off into the distance. It was early evening, the time of day when the sun was so low on the horizon it backlit the grass and the trees, turning the edges of the leaves in vineyard into neon stripes. But his dad didn't make a comment. Instead, he held his tongue, seeming to be content to sit with Shane in companionable silence, although what he was looking at, Shane didn't know.

"You want to know what I thought about just before I went into the hospital?"

His dad hadn't said a whole lot about his surgery other than to express surprise that Shane had decided to stick around. He'd been his typical sarcastic self back then, and Shane had been tempted to make a rude comment back but he hadn't. He'd stuck by his dad's side.

"I wondered if I'd worked so hard all my life just to die from a weak heart."

Shane rubbed his brow. His dad had never said a word about how he felt about his health problems. As far as Shane knew, he'd bulldozed his way through it like he did everything in life.

"But you didn't die," Shane pointed out. "You're here and getting healthier by the day."

His dad met his gaze, his blue eyes so intense Shane wondered if he'd done something wrong. Had he left the water on in one of the cattle pens? Put a horse away sweaty? Forgotten to ride one?

"God probably took one look at me and said, 'No, thanks. He can go back to Earth.'"

The words were as close to humility as he'd ever heard his father say. His dad lived life with what some might call an innate sense of entitlement, all stemming from a work ethic that'd brought him to the top of his sport…several sports. Shane would have thought his dad would expect God to roll out the red carpet for his arrival.

"It was probably more like, 'Oh, HELL no,'" Shane muttered.

He'd never joked around with his dad, and he tensed as he waited for a harsh retort. To his absolute shock, his dad seemed to smile. He couldn't tell if it was a real smile, though, because it was so small it was almost nonexistent.

"You want to know what I thought when I woke up?"

Shane just held his tongue. He'd never seen his dad in

such a contemplative mood. Not even after the surgery. He'd gone right back to usual bossy self. That day outside the arena when Kait had arrived, he'd come down to tell him that he was riding all wrong.

"First thing was how it didn't seem fair that I would wake up and your mom didn't."

The words floored him. He and his dad had never really talked about how his mom had died during an emergency surgery to remove a large mass. Frankly, when he'd heard his dad would need an operation he'd wanted to discuss it with him, about how he feared he might lose both parents in the same way, but he hadn't wanted to voice his fears out loud. Plus his mom had been terribly ill when she'd been admitted to the hospital.

"Mom's case was different."

"Yeah, but you were right the other day. I should have been there with her. I should have been the one to see her through her health problems."

"We all understood—"

"No. Don't try and excuse it for me. It's not right."

It was so strange to hear his dad apologize for something he didn't know what to say.

"The second thing I thought was, 'Where's Shane?' I had something to tell you, you see, but you weren't allowed in the recovering room. Not yet, at least. The nurses told me that, but you were the first thing on my mind when I work up."

If his dad had told him he was headed back to the rodeo circuit, he couldn't have been more surprised. He had four other siblings, and despite the fact that his dad butted heads with all of them, Shane figured his dad liked him least of all. That was a terrible thing to say, but it was true. He'd analyzed his relationship with his dad enough times that he knew it was one of the reasons he tried so hard to please him. Even after all these years, he still wanted Reese Gillian's approval.

"Why?"

His stared down into the valley again.

"I've done a lot of things in life that I'm not proud of, son. Might surprise you to know that one of those things has to do with your mom. I know it wasn't just you that disapproved of me and how I stayed away from home when she was sick. And I know of all my boys, I'm hardest on you. But the truth of the matter is I loved your mom. So much so that I couldn't bear to watch her die."

Shane stared at his dad in shock. From the veranda came the sound of laughter. Probably Carson clowning it up. Shane barely noticed. He was too busy studying his dad's eyes. They were sad and contemplative and full of regret, and he'd never seen him look that way when talking about his mom.

"I know you thought Mom and I had a combustive relationship, and the truth is, we did. I'm harder on the people I love. Don't know why. Just am. So while you might think my marriage to your mother wasn't perfect or that I regretted marrying her at times, that wouldn't be true. It was good as it could be. Your mom understood me. She stood by my side through all the years on the rodeo circuit. She put up with my bad temper and my mood swings and the times I lost it and treated her like shit. She *got* me, and when she got sick I couldn't deal with it. Plain and simple. I turned into a coward."

"She never complained."

His nodded. "She wouldn't. That's the kind of woman she was. Brave. Like your Kait."

Shane didn't know what to say. All this time he'd thought his dad didn't like Kait.

"Dad, when Kait showed up here, you seemed so afraid." Shane took a deep breath. "Why?"

His dad shrugged. "Because the moment I saw her, I knew I'd been wrong. Here was this woman pregnant with your kids, and she'd just flown all the way across the country to talk to you. And then later, I heard her talking to you, and she didn't try and guilt you into going back to her home state. No. She came to tell you she loved you. That's just like something your mom would do."

Shane's eyes burned and he realized he wanted to cry.

"That's what surgery taught me, son." His dad stared at him intently. "It's not gold buckles or winning the average at the national championships or how much money you make. It's the people in your life. I don't know why I didn't see that before, when your mother was alive." He shrugged. "Maybe I needed to stare death in the eyes. Don't know. All I know is there I was in the recovery room and I wasn't thinking about your sister and how she nearly made a mess of her life. Or your brother Carson and the fact that he doesn't have a serious bone in his body. Or Maverick and how much he wants to take over the ranch. Or Flynn and how he doesn't want a thing to do with the ranch. All I could think about was you and that girl and how much I'd tried to push you away from her and that I was wrong. I shouldn't have done that because if things are as serious between the two of you as I think they are, you shouldn't let someone like me get in the way. Someone who's made a mess of his own relationships, including the ones with his kids."

Shane leaned back. He had to blink to stop himself from crying. Had to inhale sharply. Had to clench his hands in his lap.

"So there's my spiel. Been meaning to talk to you about it since that day Kait showed up here, but I think I hoped you and Kait might work things out on your own. Didn't want you to think I'd gone soft or something. But then you came back from North Carolina still moping around, clearly crazy in love with that woman, so I thought I should probably say something."

In love?

"Don't look so shocked," his dad said. "You know you are. You might not want to admit it. After the number I've done on you about women and what a pain they are, it's not surprising you turned tail and ran, but that was my mistake, son. I see that now. If she's the one for you, go. Make it all work out. The rest of it," he waved a hand. "Your rodeo career, money, where you'll live, it's not important. *She's* important. And so are those babies. My surgery made me realize that. I hope you realize it, too."

Chapter Twenty-Three

It had been the day from hell.

She'd lost her keys in the morning. She'd walked outside on her way to the race shop only to spot a broken sprinkler spewing all over the place. When she'd climbed in her car, she'd noticed at some point a rock had hit her windshield, cracking it. So now she had a spiderweb-like pattern making its way toward the dash. And now, when she was finally back at home after a long day at the office, she couldn't seem to recall her own damn gate code. It frustrated the heck out of her, these annoying side effects of pregnancy. Thanks to her elevated hormone levels, she now had the nose of a bloodhound and the addled memory of a senior citizen.

"Damn it." She was sure she used the right code and tried it one more time.

The gate opened.

She almost cried out in glee. All she wanted to do was go inside and put her swollen feet up. Maybe take a bath, not that she wanted to see her body naked. She had come to the conclusion that some women were made to carry a baby. She wasn't one of them. Granted, she was having twins, but she'd seen pictures online of other women in the same boat. They didn't look nearly as big as she did. It wasn't fair.

Her house smelled like Christmas, thanks to the pine-scented wax she'd put in a burner. The thought reminded her that she'd be a mommy then, and, though she tried not to panic, it was hard not to wonder how she'd do it all. There were times, like today, when she couldn't imagine chasing after two young kids.

"Hello, Kait."

She jumped and dropped her keys. "What the—"

Shane stepped out of her kitchen, all dark smoldering cowboy again with his black hat.

"Shane!"

Why, oh, why, did she want to cry seeing him standing there? Why did she feel such an overwhelming urge to go to him, to crawl into his arms, to close her eyes and let him carry the weight of her world?

"You look tired."

Oh, great. Just what she wanted to hear. "Thanks."

She bent down, wincing a bit, holding her back, and picked up her keys. When she straightened, he was there in front of her, his eyes holding a softness she'd never seen before.

"How did you get in?" Come to think of it, how had he known her gate code?

"Your mom gave me a key."

"Oh, um." She motioned toward her family room. "Would you like to sit down?"

What to say? What to do? Seeing him standing there when she wasn't prepared for him brought it all back. Her pain and heartache and fears and disappointment. She didn't want him here, would kill her mother for letting him in, because she couldn't stand looking into his eyes and not—

"Kait." He reached out and touched her cheek. "I've been such a fool."

She froze. His thumb stroked the line of her jaw—back and forth, back and forth—and it made her want to close her eyes, but she couldn't look away from him. Didn't want to stop staring into his eyes.

"Why are you here?"

He smiled. "To tell you I love you."

She couldn't move, wondred if she'd heard him right.

"To admit that I was scared."

"Of what?" She tipped her head into his hand, having to close her lids as tight as possible because she did not want to cry.

"Of moving. Of starting over. Of being man enough to hold on to a woman like you."

She had to see, had to look into his eyes again to confirm that what he told her was echoed in his eyes, and when she did finally take a peek, she could barely breathe. It was all there. The love. The uncertainty. The apology she'd been hoping for but had never hoped to see or hear.

"I think we've both been scared."

He nodded. She told herself to breathe. "But you, darling Kait, are so much braver than me. I ride bulls, yet I couldn't face my fears about loving you. I let you down."

He had. Terribly. But it was okay now because he was here standing in front of her.

"I'm so sorry."

And apologizing, and she would forgive him for anything as long as he kept staring down at her with so much love in his eyes. Well, almost anything.

"It's okay."

"No, it's not." His other hand came up. He gently clasped her head, tilting it up. "I love you. I have for weeks now, but then we went to that race and I realized you could have anyone in the world. You're Kait Cooper, famous race-car driver, more amazing than any other woman in the world. I still can't believe you want me, even now standing in front of you and seeing that love in your eyes."

"Don't be afraid."

"I tried not to be. I told myself that your fame didn't matter, but it did. It messed with my head. I wanted to take care of you, but that weekend I realized you could take care of yourself. That you were such an amazingly strong-willed woman that I would never be man enough to hold you. Or so I thought."

He kissed her forehead. She closed her eyes again.

"Then I saw you at that doctor's appointment and you held my hand when we found out we were having a boy and a girl, and I knew in that moment that you *did* need me. That we were man and wife. Mother and father. Shane plus Kait."

He pulled her to him, holding her tight, and from nowhere came a smile. And tears and joy because she understood what he was trying to say.

"Our hearts are one." She felt him nod.

"You need me because I love you. Not because of who you are, but because of who you are to *me*. Just Kait. My darling Kait."

She tipped her head back, and he found her lips and then he was kissing her and she realized it wasn't a dream. This was her life. Her future. Her love.

"I love you," he whispered against her lips.

"I know," she said, because she'd always known. From that first night in Vegas to their last time together, she'd known. Deep in her heart, the realization had been there, she'd just been the first to put a name to it.

"Marry me?" he asked.

She drew back and through eyes gone blurry with tears said, "We're already married."

"For real this time. Without Elvis and the fake flowers and with our family. Our *whole* family."

She was nodding, and then he was kissing her again, and she realized that getting pregnant hadn't been a mistake. Far from it. It'd been the biggest blessing in her life—

"Ouch."

She drew back, her hand covering her belly.

"What is it?"

"I think I was just kicked." She went still, flinching a bit when it happened again. "Shane, they're moving. Feel."

He put his hand where she indicated, pressing, both of them waiting, breathless, and then she felt it again, that odd tickling sensation that was part muscle spasm, part gas bubble but oh so special.

"I feel it."

He stared at her in awe. She smiled and then he kissed her again and she kissed him back, and then they were laughing and smiling and holding on to each other as if they would never let go.

Epilogue

Kait shot up in bed.

"Shane," she cried just before she gasped again. "Shane!"

Shane rolled over in bed, took one look at her face in the dusky half-light of dawn and knew. She could tell by the way his eyes went wide.

"It's time?"

She nodded, clutching a belly as big as a horse's. She would know, too. Despite Shane's objections, she'd insisted on moving back to California with him, living in the old ranch house until their own home could be built on Gillian acreage.

"Call my mom and dad."

Shane jumped out of bed. Kait winced as she slowly shifted to the side of the bed. It was truly amazing how much a female belly could stretch. She half joked that she needed a sling to hold it up. The doctor had said everything was normal, but there was nothing "normal" about not being able to see her own feet.

A contraction hit again. She gasped.

"Okay, I don't know who came up with the idea of childbirth, but I can tell right now this is going to be bunk."

"My mom told me when I was little that God had to be a man because childbirth would never have been invented by a woman."

"She's right." She flinched again. "This baby's coming soon."

"Then we better get going. Your mom and dad said they will meet us at the hospital." Shane thrust a jug of orange juice toward her. He held a a robe in the other hand. "I called Dr. Penrod, too. He's on his way."

"What is that for?"

He stared down at his hands as if surprised to see he held something. "I thought you might be thirsty."

She laughed, but it was choked off by another contraction. "I'm not wearing a robe to the hospital."

"But you might need it later."

She just shook her head. "Fine."

They were on their way in record time, which was a good thing because all Kait wanted was drugs, especially after having to hoist herself into Shane's truck. She was pretty sure she'd pulled some muscles on the way up.

She tried to distract herself during the drive, staring at the trees and the hills around them. Her parents had been incredible about her move to California. When she'd explained that she liked the anonymity that went along with living in a state that had nothing to do with racing, they'd packed up their bags and moved west, too. Well, not everything. There was now Cooper Racing West and East. Once the babies came, Kait would operate out of Cooper Racing West while her brother operated out of their East Coast facility. She couldn't believe her parents would do that for her but they had, and she would forever be grateful.

"Almost there."

She clutched the door handle thanks to another jolt of pain. "Dear God, what did women do before epidurals?"

"Screamed a lot."

"Right now I'd cut my own spinal cord if it meant not feeling this pain."

Shane's lips twitched, but she could have sworn he sped up, and that was good. Her husband did a great imitation of a stock-car driver when he screeched to a stop beneath the hospital's portico. She would barely recall being helped out of Shane's truck or sinking into a wheelchair. Her eyes were closed the whole time, mostly because she was wincing so much from pain.

"This is ridiculous," she said as they helped her into a bed. "I mean, seriously. Ridiculous."

"I know," the nurse said as she hooked her up to a fetal monitor. "I've had two kids. I couldn't imagine giving birth naturally."

Kait gasped. Shane came forward, grabbed her hand. The nurse patted her. "It's okay. Your doctor will be here any moment now. They'll get you all hooked up."

"I hope so," Kait grunted, "because I'm telling you right now, I'm about to lose it."

Poor Shane. He seemed so bewildered. She didn't care. The tears were coming, hopefully the last tears she would shed in a long time, because she was sick to death of crying. Cry, cry, cry. That was all she'd done this entire pregnancy. Well, not the last third of her pregnancy. That'd been filled with love and laughter and a happiness she wouldn't have thought possible. It'd been a crazy life, what with the move and opening up a new shop and dealing with a new place to live, but it'd been a good kind of crazy.

"So, here we are," said the kindly doctor who'd helped her all those months ago when she'd been put on bed rest. "Time to have some babies."

Dear God, please let him cut the small talk.

"Let's get your epidural started and then we'll see what we've got."

Oh, thank God.

Everything moved quickly then. She was told to roll onto her side. She would have run naked down the hall if that was what they'd wanted her to do. Soon enough she was told not to move by yet another doctor and then there was the tiniest of pinpricks, not nearly as painful as the damn contractions, and then…heaven.

"Better?" asked the anesthesiologist.

"Sooo much better," she sighed.

Her mom and dad arrived then, or maybe the doctors were just now letting them in the room. Kait didn't know, because things had really sped up. She watched as Shane and her dad greeted each other. Her dad was happy as long as she was happy, and Shane had promised to never let her down.

"Okay, let me see your arm," said the nurse. "We're going to start a drip to keep you and the babies hydrated while you labor."

She didn't think she'd need the IV long. Apparently, her twins wanted to be born now, and though she didn't feel any pain, her body still contracted and contorted and she still had to breathe and work hard.

"Almost there," said the doctor. "Keep pushing."

She felt the strangest sensation. A pressure unlike any she'd felt before. The feeling only worsened and was not painful but not exactly pleasant, either.

"Here we go. One last push. And…" Dr. Penrod said. "…it's your little girl."

Finally. Thank God. Except she had to do it again. No. She didn't want to do it again.

"Name?" asked a nurse.

"Abigail," she hear Shane say, but she was too tired to open her eyes and look.

Abigail. After his mom. Abigail Sarah Gillian.

"Okay, here we go again."

She wasn't kidding. She didn't think she could do it again, but then her body heaved and she sucked in a breath because she could feel the pressure, and she knew she had no choice. Her son was coming. Now.

"There he is," said Dr. Penrod. "One more push, Kait."

Oh, sure. Easy for him to say.

"Come on, Kait," Shane whispered. "Once more."

"Shut up," she grunted. "Just shut up and let me work."

She thought she heard Shane chuckle, or maybe it was her mom. She got up on her elbows and bore down like never before, grateful her dad had been banished from the room because it couldn't have been pretty down there. Not at all.

"One more time," she heard her mom say.

So strange how she could feel the pressure but not the pain, and then she felt…nothing. Blessed relief.

"There he is," the doctor announced.

She lay back. She wanted to sleep. For hours. Maybe days.

"Name?" she heard the nurse say from a distance.

"Lance," Shane answered.

Her mom gasped. Kait forced herself to open her

eyes to seek out her mom's familiar face, her smile strained from exhaustion.

"He'll be so touched," her mom said.

Kait nodded and closed her eyes again, but then a nurse handed her something and she realized it was her daughter. Her tiny little Abigail and she needed to push herself up again even though she didn't feel like moving.

"You need help?"

"No. I'm okay."

She wanted to see her daughter. Shane plumped up some pillows. Kait held out her hands. The nurse placed her baby girl in her waiting arms.

"Hello, sweetheart," she whispered. Oh, she was so tiny, with just the slightest little mop of dark hair and a puckered-up face that made Kait want to giggle.

Shane came up alongside her and they both stared into that funny little face that was still beautiful even though it was red from crying.

"Shh," she tried to soothe her. "Shh, shh, shh. It's okay, baby girl."

"Would you like to hold your son?" the nurse asked Shane.

He nodded mutely. In a moment their second child was placed in his arms and the two of them were huddled together with her mom looking on as, for the last time in what would be a very long while—thankfully—Kait cried. They all cried. And when Shane's family came in, there were tears in Shane's brothers' eyes and his sister's, and they all *oohed* and *aahed* over the newest member of the Gillian family.

It was a moment Kait would never forget. The first of many great moments. And later, when she married Shane for the second time—she'd refused to do so until she could fit into her wedding dress—she cemented another memory in her mind. There would be other moments like that: Shane winning the average at the NFR…the first of three times he would win it. Kait's first big win after her return to racing. The first time Abigail and Lance walked. But for Kait, the sweetest memory of all was that long ago day when Shane came to North Carolina to tell her he loved her.

He told her that all the time now. He would tell her that for all the days to come…for the rest of their lives.

* * * * *

If you loved this novel, look for
Pamela Britton's previous books in her
COWBOYS IN UNIFORM *series:*

HER RODEO HERO
HIS RODEO SWEETHEART
THE RANGER'S RODEO REBEL
HER COWBOY LAWMAN
WINNING THE RANCHER'S HEART

Available now from Harlequin.com!

We hope you enjoyed this story from
Harlequin® Western Romance.

Harlequin® Western Romance is coming to an end, but community, cowboys and true love are here to stay. Starting July 2018, discover more heartfelt tales of family and friendship from **Harlequin® Special Edition**.

Romance is for life, and these stories show that every chapter in a relationship has its challenges and delights and that love can be renewed with each turn of the page!

Look for six *new* romances every month
from **Harlequin® Special Edition!**
Available wherever books are sold.

COMING NEXT MONTH FROM

⟨H⟩ HARLEQUIN®

Western Romance

Available April 3, 2018

#1685 THE TEXAS COWBOY'S BABY RESCUE
Texas Legends: The McCabes
by Cathy Gillen Thacker
When nurse Bridgett Monroe finds an abandoned newborn baby, everyone thinks Cullen Reid McCabe is the father. But this honest cowboy is determined to find the child's real family—with Bridgett's help.

#1686 COWBOY SEAL DADDY
Cowboy SEALs • by Laura Marie Altom
Paisley Carter has been burned by love, but pregnancy hormones have her crushing on her sexy SEAL pretend fiancé! Then a weekend on Wayne's ranch has Paisley thinking she and Wayne should unite for real.

#1687 REUNITED WITH THE BULL RIDER
Gold Buckle Cowboys • by Christine Wenger
Callie Wainwright romanced cowboy Reed Beaumont in their youth, but his burgeoning career as a bull rider called a halt to their happily-ever-after. But the boy is back in town, and the sparks between them are as hot as ever.

#1688 THE COWBOY'S SURPRISE BABY
Spring Valley, Texas • by Ali Olson
Amy McNeal broke Jack Stuart's heart back in high school. Now she's pregnant, and they have to get over their painful past and try to be a family—for the baby's sake.

YOU CAN FIND MORE INFORMATION ON UPCOMING HARLEQUIN® TITLES, FREE EXCERPTS AND MORE AT WWW.HARLEQUIN.COM.

HWESTCNM0318

*Could Bridgett Monroe's shocking discovery soften the
notoriously rigid Cullen McCabe?*

*Read on for a sneak preview of
THE TEXAS COWBOY'S BABY RESCUE,
the first book in Cathy Gillen Thacker's series
TEXAS LEGENDS: THE MCCABES.*

Cullen McCabe slammed to a halt just short of her.

His dark brows lowered like thunderclouds over
mesmerizing blue eyes. Her breath caught in her chest.

"Is this an April Fool's joke?" he demanded gruffly.

Suddenly feeling angry, Bridgett gestured at the sleeping
infant beyond the nursery's glass window. The adorable
newborn had curly espresso brown hair and gorgeous blue
eyes.

Just like the man in front of her.

"Does this look like a joke, McCabe?" Because it sure
wasn't to Bridgett, who'd found the abandoned baby.

Their eyes clashed, held for an interminably long
moment. Cullen looked back, lingering on the tag attached
to the infant bed: Robby Reid McCabe.

"What do I have to do with this baby? Other than that we
apparently share the same last name?"

Bridgett reached into the pocket of her scrubs and
withdrew the rumpled envelope. "This was left beside the
fire station along with the child."

With a scowl, he opened the envelope, pulled out the
typewritten paper and read out loud, "Cullen, I know

you never planned to have a family or get married, and I understand that, but please be the daddy little Robby deserves."

Reacting like he'd landed on some crazy reality TV show, Cullen looked around suspiciously.

To no avail. The only cameras were the security ones the hospital employed. As Cullen stepped closer to the glass and gave the baby another intent look, Bridgett inched nearer and stared up at him. At six foot four, he towered over her.

"You found him?"

She nodded.

Cullen's expression radiated compassion. "I'm sorry to hear that." His voice dropped. "But unfortunately, I don't have any connection to this baby."

"Sure about that?"

He frowned at her. "Think I'd know if I'd conceived a child with someone."

"Not necessarily," she countered. Not if he hadn't been told.

Briefly, a deep resentment seemed to flicker in his gaze.

He lowered his face to hers and spoke in a masculine tone that sent a thrill down her spine. "I'd know if I'd slept with someone in the last ten months or so."

He paused to let that sink in. "Obviously, you don't believe me."

Bridgett shrugged. "It's not up to me to believe you or not." This was becoming too personal, too fast.

Don't miss THE TEXAS COWBOY'S BABY RESCUE by Cathy Gillen Thacker, available April 2018 wherever Harlequin® Western Romance books and ebooks are sold.

www.Harlequin.com

Looking for more satisfying love stories
with community and family at their core?

Check out **Harlequin® Special Edition**
and **Harlequin® Western Romance** books!

New books available every month!

CONNECT WITH US AT:

Harlequin.com/Community

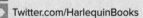 Facebook.com/HarlequinBooks

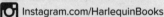 Twitter.com/HarlequinBooks

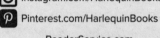 Instagram.com/HarlequinBooks

Pinterest.com/HarlequinBooks

ReaderService.com

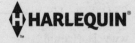

**ROMANCE WHEN
YOU NEED IT**

HFGENRE2017R